# Reaching For Reveries

A historical novel

The Sagacity Stories Series

Book 2

By Jennifer Toelle

This book is a blend of both fiction and history. The author, Jennifer Toelle is versed in history, biography, and curation and is a meticulous researcher of historic context and data. The protagonist, Sena, inspired by a true story, anchors the fictional narrative. The narrative is a piece of fiction crafted by the author's imagination. For narrative cohesion certain details have been included to fill in the gaps where historic records stop and imagination begins.

The retention of original historical names of people and places serves to immerse the reader in a historical backdrop, notably the Montana cities of Butte, Missoula, Great Falls and Helena during the years spanning 1900 to 1907; 1948 in California with well known national names and headline news events in the United States. The history celebrates the local region and its people who have contributed greatly to each community.

Refer to the character glossary at the end of this book. This section provides further biographical and contextual details about the characters.

The images contained within this book are in the public domain or are a historically inspired digital creation by the author. Pierce family photographs are courtesy of Patricia McGrath Snipes. For digital creation, the author used imaging software, such as, Adobe Firefly.

Special thanks to the members of my Writer's Collective for their steadfast support throughout the writing and editing process. I'm deeply grateful to my family and friends who patiently listened to countless hours of book details. And to Valerie and Mary Jane—thank you for your thoughtful insight.



Janine Chellington Press. L.L.C. | Central Kansas.

ISBN: 979-8-9906048-2-7
LCCN: 2025906256

# Forward

**Protagonist Notes From Beyond...**

At some point, I stopped trusting joy. I yearned for joy, because there was an absence of it from my childhood. I learned that joy seemed as fleeting as smoke in the wind, gone just when I thought I had it clenched tight.

Fleeting, fickle joy! It teased me, jostling in a pristine well, only for a storm to churn the water into murky muck. Life can swiftly turn sour without warning.

I spent years chasing dreams, grasping for some divine light, daring to believe that happiness, real happiness, was within reach. For brief moments, I soared, weightless, in the thrill of my reverie. But just as quickly, I plummeted, as if joy itself had betrayed me. I thought of it as the servers at dinner parties circling with tantalizing tastes of scrumptious hors d'oeuvres. Too many bites leading to sickly pangs in my gut.

My mind is a labyrinth of past lives, dragging me through memories I have often tried to forget. No matter how hard I shove them into the shadows, they lurk, stubborn as an awful song that gets stuck in your head. There have been so many moments when I wanted to talk to someone about them, I couldn't. Everyone from my past has disappeared, just like the joy I kept losing my grip on. Each time I started over, I left them behind, along with the pieces of myself I no longer needed.

I could, after all, revisit the past in a pinch—when needing a favor or facing a difficult situation. Fate had left me lonely, bereft of any support system, time and time again. I longed for connection; perhaps dreaming of joy is what I yearned for during this period of my life—a deep desire to belong, to connect, or to have a memory to cling to in the lonely hours. Sometimes my past crept up like nightmares—the past colliding with the hopes I once had for the future.

Get ready to read about an adventurous period in my life! One thing is for certain, I was always reaching for reveries.

— Sena

# Recap of Book 1
# Zoetic Solace

In the mid-1890s, Sena, a Swedish immigrant and teenager, travels to Helena, Montana, to reunite with her mother. In her search, she encounters the wealthy Holter family, who takes her in as a domestic servant. The lines between servant and daughter blur as they treat her like their own and insist she would attend high school. They strive to protect her from her alcoholic mother, who has remarried a physically abusive husband and has more children.

When the Holters depart for California, Sena moves in with her best friend's family. During this time, her mother divorces her stepfather and persuades Sena to move to Butte, Montana. There, she discovers that her mother is involved with her ex-husband's brother, a saloon and dance hall owner, leading to further drama. Her mother leaves with another man for San Francisco.

In Butte, Sena meets Owen, a dashing vaudeville comedian, and becomes naively caught up in a whirlwind romance. However, a mere 11 days into their marriage, Owen disappears, leaving her heartbroken and alone, yet again.

Book 1: *Zoetic Solace's* storyline spans from 1895 to 1900, with bookends offering glimpses of Sena's life in an unspecified location in 1962.

In Book 2: *Reaching for Reveries* the narrative continues from 1900 to 1907, with bookends set in 1948.

# Celebrating Local History

The purpose of this series extends beyond telling a story about a woman; it aims to celebrate local history.

Each place has a unique story for its residents, both on an individual level and collectively. In the book, *Defining Memory*, David E. Kyvig, distinguished research professor, articulates how defining a sense of place brings deeper meaning:

> Whether passed on in the form of oral tradition, publications, or collections of objects, the localized past is a vital component of the identity of a place. It holds interest for both residents and those who visit the place for the first time. When, as often happens, people talk of their "roots," they refer to a personal identity that sinks deep into the soil of a place.

Our protagonist steps foot and plants herself upon many pieces of soil. With each new book in the series, another city is explored. The Sagacity Stories series takes readers on a journey across the United States, featuring locations such as Missoula and Billings, Montana; Deadwood and Hot Springs, South Dakota; Jacksonville, Florida; Denver, Colorado; Kansas City, Missouri; McPherson, Kansas; Casper, Wyoming; Los Angeles, San Diego, and San Francisco, California; and Seattle, Washington, as well as many other fascinating places.

Readers will have the joy of immersing themselves in the local history and discover how our protagonist, Sena, navigates these locations and how she interacts with different people.

It's all based on a true story.

# Table of Contents

**Chapter 10**

*March 1902:  Missoula, Montana*..................................81

**Chapter 11**

*April 1902:  Missoula, Montana*.............................. 97

**Chapter 12**

*May 1902:  Missoula, Montana*............................. 109

*October 1902:  Missoula, Montana* ...................... 113

**Chapter 13**

*Butte, Montana*........................................ 115

*Missoula, Montana*....................................117

*From Franklin J. Pierce's Perspective*
*January 1903: Missoula Montana* ...........................119

*February 1903: Missoula Montana* ....................... 123

**Chapter 14**

*From Franklin J. Pierce's Perspective*
*March 1903: Missoula, Montana* ........................... 129

*May 1903: Missoula, Montana*............................... 131

*June 1903: Missoula, Montana*............................. 134

**Chapter 15**

*From Franklin J. Pierce's Perspective*
*June 1903: Missoula, Montana*...........................137

*July 1903: Missoula, Montana* ........................... 138

*August 1903: Missoula, Montana* .......................... 144

*September 1903: Missoula, Montana* ..................... 145

**Chapter 16**

*Returning to Sena's Perspective*
*September 1903:  Missoula, Montana* ................. 149

*May 1904: Houston, Texas*........................... 157

*Summer 1904: Texas Coastline* ........................... 159

**Chapter 17**

*1904 to 1905: Traveling Western US*
*December 1904: Missoula, Montana*................... 164

*January 1905: Missoula, Montana* ....................... 170

Vaudeville's Struggle for Respectability............... 172

# Chapter 1

**January 1948, age 68, California**

The Telechron radio alarm clock dings, sending music waves rippling through the air to the polka tune, *Toolie, Oolie, Doolie*, by the Andrew Sisters.

Sena sighs, places a hand on the sleeping mask, and stretches her hand toward the alarm clock, slamming an index finger and pressing the top button down as the Andrews Sisters sing the phrase, "alpine moon." Another sigh escapes as a hand clasps the forehead, chronic catarrh and aching sinus cavities making their presence known. Re-closing her eyelids, tilting her head to the left, to the right, deep sighs echoing in the morning's stillness. Hearing cars pass by adds to the agony of her throbbing head. The newspaper's thud on the door makes her jump; the sudden noise jolts her. Wincing, she presses her fingers on the bridge of her nose, squeezing tightly for relief.

Slinking her body upward amid her discomfort, caressing her silk head wrap neatly tied in a bow around the base of her head. The softness soothes her. As her feet touch the floor, she wiggles her toes, her usual habit, she searches for her slippers without looking.

Shuffling her way to the bathroom, trying to hold back the nausea from the phlegm moving through her throat.

Opening the medicine cabinet, she reaches for the Kloronol bottle, spraying it into her nostrils to unclog her nose. Muttering, "Damn catarrh!" And sighs. Reaching for her trusty Elys Cream Balm she has used for decades. Applying makeup was difficult with the gnawing ache in her face. As the morning went on, the pain eased.

Entering the kitchen, turning the radio dial on, she hears the announcer mentioning the Chinese New Year. Staring out the window preparing her morning meal, she reels up that memory. This brings back one of those complicated memories in her life— one evoking a mix of elated joy and great pain.

After eating breakfast, grabbing her petite briefcase, she hunts for her keys. Spotting the keys, Yara leaps onto the table. Scooping up the cat in her arms, giving her ears a good scratch and a gentle stroke down the back. Gently placing cat on the floor, whispering, "there you go, Yara," changing her vocal tone to sternness, "now stay off the table."

Driving through the newly developed suburbia, she cruises over to the pier and parks along the boardwalk. Spotting her glamorous friend, she waves, "Hiya, Mae!"

Through the hazy morning sun, Mae lifts her arm in a graceful arc, waving back. "Hi, Sena, darling!" Mae continues her stroll down the boardwalk, finishing up her routine morning walk.

Sena calls out, "Have a swell day on the set!"

Mae gives a stylish nod, flipping her hand in the air, exuding the confidence of a movie star. "Always do, doll!"

Sena grabs her briefcase and makes her way to a yacht docked along the pier. The vessel gleams with polished wood and chrome accents, the streamlined design a nod to modern luxury. As she boards, her hand glides over the smooth, varnished mahogany rail, the coolness of the metal trim a refreshing contrast that soothes the nagging sinus headache that has been bugging her. The yacht exudes an air of sophistication. The yacht's sleek lines mirror her as a floating symbol of refinement.

"This way, ma'am," says a man in uniform, guiding her to the deck. "Wait here. Someone will be with you shortly."

Standing upon the deck, Sena takes in the crisp morning air as they set off into the Pacific. The expanse of the sea encircles her, feeling similar to cogs in a gigantic machine.

A tall, rugged man steers the ship. This reminds her of an old friend. He nods at her — she cannot resist reeling up a memory. Images of her memory appear in her mind like watching herself through a dreamy souvenir snow globe. A vision of her younger self smiling in the peppering snow with friends in a sleigh.

"Sena, I've prepared--" comes a voice from behind.

Sena quickly straightens up, smoothing her hair and clasping her hands properly in front of her. "Oh, Ms. Welling, hello. Isn't it a peach of a morning, especially for January?"

"Oh yah, livin' out here sure has its perks! I was talkin' to my sister in Minnesota just yesterday—oh, don't ya know, they're freezin' up there!" Ms. Welling says, glancing down at her clipboard. "I've got a nice selection of tablecloths and linens for ya to pick from. And I've lined up a couple of chefs with some sample meals and desserts for ya to try—just divine, they are! Sure to be the talk of the town at your event. Now, if ya wanna follow me, we'll head on over to the dining room and dance hall. Small, cozy—perfect for the small dinner party."

As they enter the dance hall, Sena's eyes linger on the stage, feeling a heightened sense of déjà vu with a delicate mix of comfort and unease—complicated masks emotions. The spotlight, the attention, the wild adventures of her youth—all hidden at the bottom of the well, where no one can see.

"Oh yah, we've got top-notch entertainment, the best performers you'll find anywhere," Ms. Welling continues as they make their way to the dining room. "And about your dinner party at home, I've put together a real nice list of catering options for ya," handing her the list. "Now, back to the yacht party. If I got this right, this little shindig is for a Chinese New Year celebration, eh?" asks Miss Welling.

"Yes, this space is simply divine, perfect for our event. And thank you for the catering suggestions. Ja am to host a dinner party soon at my home. I have Swedish royalty on the guest list. Everything must be just right. I intend to be the most divine hostess imaginable."

**Summer 1900, age 20, Butte, Montana**
*In the following dialogue, characters may speak in a blend of their native languages and dialects, such as, Swedish, French and Irish, blending their newly learned English.*

Seated, Sena sits waiting outside an office door.

The door swings open, a young man comes out, "Ma'am, she vill see you now."

Sena stands up slowly, cautiously, and walks into the room where she sees Madame Paumie, impeccably fashionable and businesslike, staring down at a piece of paper.

Paumie continuing to look down, "Have a seat."

Sena sits, her anxiety showing clearly on her face.

"I am told you are alone?" asks Paumie.

"Ja, Ma'am," Sena politely responds.

"That your husband has deserted you?" Paumie questions Sena.

Sena looks down, filled with shame, and nods, avoiding eye contact. "Ja, Ma'am."

"Alors, what are you to do about this?" Paumie presses, her tone assertive.

Sena fidgets with her hands, then looks up. After a moment of awkward silence, she quietly says, "I plan to file for what they call, eh, a divorce. Ja need, eh, means."

Paumie places the paper down on her desk and leans back in her chair, looking Sena piercingly in the eyes. "I see, et you want to work here for me. You understand zis is no frill, no fancy job. We create elaborate and fancy materials, yet ze work requires créativité, determination, and grit."

Sena eagerly nods. "Ja, Ma'am," realizing her Swedish creeping in, corrects herself, "I, Ma'am" for she feels intimidated by this strong business woman with a French accent.

Paumie assumingly says, "It's okay to have our native languages creepin' back into tongues. It's a plethora of languages 'round here."

Sena nods.

Paumie questioning, "I hear you learn quickly, et you are a hard worker?"

"Ja, Ma'am. I assure you, I vill work diligently," says Sena.

"You did not list any references. What work, have you for, eh, expérience de travail? Work experience?"

Sena looks around the room nervously, grappling to find the words under pressure. "I have worked as a domestic for the Holters in Helena—"

Paumie cuts her off—"The Holters? I see, how long?"

"Three years, Ma'am. I cooked, cleaned, laundry, read—"

"*Read*?" Paumie asks curiously.

"Ja, read. The Holters required me to attend high school."

"Did you graduate?" Madame Paumie questions.

"No, almost." Sena responds.

"I see. You are literate, oui or non?" Asks Paumie.

"Oh, ja, ja. I was a remarkable pupil in Helena. My teacher, Miss Sanders, says I was brilliant," Sena asserting, "Miss Knowles Haskell says I am—" struggling to find the words then pronouncing it perfectly in English, "articulate."

"Oh! You know Ella? My attorney?" Paumie questions in a surprised tone. "You see Ella about dat divorce!"

Sena nods and looks down anxiously. Thinking about her mother's divorce. Ella Haskell-Knowles represented her mother, and it did not go well.

"Hmmm," Paumie hands Sena a piece of paper. "Given zis order, how much fabric do we need to create zis dress? Also, tally ze price."

After examining the paper for two minutes, she looks up, "150 yards needed. If extra is required for tassels, decoration or any errors, Ja gest more yards for extra. The total cost of this order here," pointing down at the paper, "would be $58.50. Will there be tax?"

"Oui, oui, brillante, indeed! Your computation in your head, without un instrument." Madame Paumie taps her pencil. "Do you have a desire to learn how to dye material Parisian methods?"

"Ja, I vould love to learn!" Sena exclaims, her eyes widening, then realizing her over-enthusiasm, she straightens and regains composure.

*Paumie's Parisian Dye House, c1895.*
*West Galena Street, Butte, Montana*

Madame Paumie raises an eyebrow. "Bien. You report here Monday. Now, Sena, is it? Do you have housing?"

Embarrassment washes over Sena's face. She looks down, not making eye contact. "Ma'am, no, they evicted me."

"Très bien, I have quarters available. You may stay in my building. I'll dock ze rent from your pay. You must have a safe place to reside. C'est la seule façon. I also do not want vermin, pests, or anything of ze sort touching my business. Oui? No libations, no recklessness. Zis is a business."

"Oh, thank you, Ma'am, thank you!"

"Oui, oui." Madame Paumie lifts her hands.

Sena bursts into Galena Street, a gritty, dirty layer of dust clinging to the beautiful, bustling Butte, where gold glimmers in the minds of all. Looking towards the mountains, tilting her head to the skyline, gratitude overflows as she raises her hands and twirls right there in the street. Suddenly, a man's voice—comedically reminiscent of Owen's—startles her. She stumbles into him, and they both tumble to the ground. Disappointment flickers; it is not Owen. If it were, she would stammer but still give him a piece of her mind for leaving her destitute. Yet, she finds herself mesmerized by this man's charming smile.

Extending a hand to help her up, "ah, lass, if I'd known twirlin' was all it took to sweep ya off your feet, I'd have joined in. Forgive me, I must've been wanderin' 'round with me head in the clouds instead of watchin' me step."

"Thank you," she says dusting herself off and sighing.

"Say, lass, I'm Frank S. Gates, comedian at your service," moving his hands around. "You should come catch me in a show down the street."

"Damn!" She thought. Another vaudeville comedian trying to worm his way in and charm her, just like Owen did...

# Chapter 2

**Summer 1900, Butte, Montana**

Speckles of dust on the floor siphon up as Sena dashes across the dye room to deliver the orders she had just taken.

"Here you go." She says handing it off to the lead supervisor.

As she climbs the stairs, she sees Frank bundled up outside on the sidewalk smoking a cigar, his breath making circles in the air. Was he waiting for her? No, she would NOT fall for charming wit like she had with Owen. No way, no how! She grabs her coat as Madame Paumie steps out of her office. "Oh, Miss Bjork?"

"Yes, Madame Paumie?" Sena asks.

"Did you get all the orders in?" Madame. Paumie asks.

"Yes, Madame." Sena replies.

"Did you get the black silk ordered? You know we need it by the end of the month," Madame Paumie states in a matter-of-fact tone.

Sena nods, "Yes, Madame, all ordered."

Madame acknowledges, "Very well. You zis a good evening."

Frank spotted her as she departs the dye house, coming over to her like a jack-in-the box. The spring in his step, ever so bouncy. "Hello there, lass!"

Sena kept her head high and kept walking trying not to acknowledge him. He was charming. Every theater crowd adores him before he mutters his joke of the day.

"C'mon, lass look at me, hear me out and I'll be on my way.," Frank says convincingly.

She stops and turns towards him against her better judgment.

"All right, that's more like it, lass. So, I hear you know your way around a theater."

"No, no, no!" Her eyes widen, her body tenses, and tears well. Her anger begins to boil over.

"Lass, calm down. I am not that Owen character who left you high and dry. Besides, me has a wife. She's not here, and I'll be divorcing her soon..." Chuckles "Kinda got ta live in the same town to be married. Dinna worry, I'm not interested in playing house with you."

Sena walks off and rolls her eyes to the clouds.

Frank scurries after her. "Lass, we need you at the theater tonight."

Sena stops and lets out a deep sigh. "Whatever for?"

"Ahh, lass, I knew you'd come around!" He locks his arm inside hers and says, "Lulu will be so excited."

Sena enters the theater. She secretly has missed this place. She hears Lulu squealing, "Sena!" Before being able to utter a word, Lulu sprints to Sena and engulfs her arms around her and hugs her tightly.

Lulu says, "Oh! We so desperately need you. This place will dazzle again!"

Breaking from the embrace, Kittie and Sena exchange waves from across the room. The smells of perfume, liquor and cigar smoke permeates the room. Some actors and company take to the stage while others make themselves comfortable, as if the audience seating was their living room parlor. Sena pours herself a drink of brandy. She finds a seat next to Kittie, watching everyone's carefree nature.

**Her inner monologue:**
This brandy helps me relax, the best elixir. Musn't I drink a heap of it. I shall not end up like my mother falling prey to drunken men and being' loose, lying in beds she should not dare. I wish the advertised letters in the paper would print my name. When I saw the postmaster earlier this week, still no post for me. Why will my mother not write a few lines to assure me she is safe and well? Why have I still not heard from Owen? Am I stupid and a naïve girl? I long for him to come back. I love him; I do. I still love him. I will want to forever be Mrs. Bockley. He should be here in this theater amongst the other carefree souls. [Frank catches her eye. He is practicing his witty jokes on the stage.] Frank's comedic wit is somewhat better than Owen's, yet doesn't possess his dashing appearance.

Sena breaks from her inner monologue as Lulu sits down and says, "I'm glad you have returned to us," with a sheepish smile and placing her hands under her chin. "Have you heard any word from Owen?"

Sena takes a sip of her brandy and shakes her head no, tears welling in her eyes.

Lulu places a hand upon Sena's, tilting her head and resting it upon Sena's shoulder. Sena reciprocates.

Lulu whispers, "If there's one thing I've learned growing up around the theater life, actors are the most accepting people of other's quirks and eccentricities. They are also damn good at disguising their *true* intentions."

Tears stream down Sena's face.

Lulu continues, "My eavesdropping upon father's conversations and business dealings has turned up no news." Lulu wipes Sena's cheek, erasing the tear stream away. They both let out a cathartic laugh. "You are better off without that deceitful comedian." Lulu says assuringly.

They both chuckle as Frank yells out, "No crying in here, let's keep the laughs a rollin'!"

Later that night Sena lies in her bed staring into the darkness, she contemplates her relationship with her theater friends.

**Her inner monologue runs wild feeling as though she's floating:** I enjoy being around them, because I do not have to fit into a societal mold. Everyone was comfortable in their skin, baring all their eccentricities. Lulu's right, though. How can I trust an actor? Goodness, mercy, can I trust Lulu? Can I trust Frank? I certainly fell prey to Owen. I bared my soul. I bared my nakedness to that man. How it felt when he was inside me. How was I so naïve? I placed all my trust in him. We would have a wonderful life. [*feels something crawling across her foot*] Oh my! Disgust! I hate spiders! I shall not live like this, in this wretched place. I must find something to squash that insect to pieces! [She picks up a shoe and slams her shoe upon the spider with force. She lays back down pulling the quilted blanket that Emily had given her when she left the Holter home around her.] I miss Emily. I miss the Holter's. I miss Helena. I miss the circular staircase. I miss the comfort of the noises in that house. Why did they not take me to California? I would have been spared all this pain with my mother and then Owen.

Tears seep, rolling down her cheek and onto the silk scrap inlaid in the quilt. Sena places her finger upon the tear-stained silk as though she is mending it. She moves her finger steadily across the seams; Each intricate, zig zagged piece of the crazy quilt. All scraps create a beautiful array of hues and colors. In the corner, "Emily" is stitched in violet thread. She traces the "E" with her finger, soothing her broken heart enough to drift off for the night.

Morning air enters the Paumie apartments via an open window. Sena walks briskly out her door and down the corridor. A man in suspenders holding a large ledger catches Sena's eye. Numerous pencils are visibly stuffed into each of the man's pockets. A pencil is also perched on his ear. "How strange," she ponders, holding a big notebook. This man is the center of attention, surrounded by her apartment neighbors. To get to work, Sena races to the dye house. "Miss Sena," a neighbor shouts, "a man needs your age and place of birth."

Sena blurts back as she scurries off. "I'm 20 years old – you give him my details!"

Speaking with the census taker, the neighbor chuckles and mentions, "She's divorced and is known to work as a prostitute."

The census taker writes zealously. "And age and native country of origin?"
Ah, one of those Scandinavian countries, about age 20."

The census taker writes down, "21" and "Norway."

Another neighbor sees the census taker writing and says, "No, I think she is from Denmark."

The census taker draws a line through Norway and writes Denmark above it. He takes the word of the neighbor that Sena is a prostitute.

Another neighbor, Greta, leans in to the lying man's ear, whispers and grits her teeth, "Sena will surely be irate! How dare you say those sinful things about her to the census, man? Don't you know, that's an official record."

Greta departs, because the census taker already has her information.  She observes Madame Paumie signaling for Sena to enter her office and assist with a custom drape order.

Frank walks Sena home in the evening shortly after meal time. As they walk up the stairs, they meet Greta, holding a basket of freshly laundered items.

Yet another neighbor, a man, gives Frank and Sena a disapproving look.

Frank yells at the man exiting, "What's gottin' in your knickers?" Greta's shoulders raise and she sighs with a telltale face of concern.

Sena's eyes widen. "What's happened?"

Greta looks away, then glances down at her laundry and back up to meet Sena's gaze. "No, I don't want to share this vulgar news with you."

Frank laughs, shaking his hands. "Oooo, vulgarities? We are so frightened."

Greta maintains a somber look. "Remember the day you scurried off, and the man was here recording information?"

Sena nods.

"Well, Melvin thought he was the jokester and told the census recorder falsities about you."

Sena's eyes narrow. "What?"

Greta continues, "Afraid so, miss. He says you were a prostitute," looking down and nervously fiddling with a piece of clothing in her basket.

"They think I am..." Gasps Sena.

"And they think I am..." Frank mimics and points a finger at his chest.

Sena and Frank burst into laughter.

As they stand in silence in the moments following, Sena's anger stirs inside her, "I would never!" Sena walks towards Melvin's room, and raises her fists pounding on his door, "MELVIN, a word!?"

Greta shakes her head calmly. "Miss Sena, I am afraid Melvin left today, went to Anaconda. Don't think the likes of him will return."

Sena nervously asks, "What type of recorder was this? Will it be printed in the newspapers?"

"No, a government recorder, for household information and the like."

Frank chimes in, "ah, the Census!"

Greta nods. "I believe so, yes. Well, best be turning in for the night. Dinna worry your head about Melvin's tales. Someone recorded it in a book and will put it on a shelf, never to see the light of day." Sena sighs and turns toward her door and back at Frank. "Thank you for walking me home."

"You're welcome, lass. Night," says Frank.

Entering her apartment, Sena places her hat on a hook. She reaches for a hairpin, followed by several more, releasing the tension in her hair. As her hair falls, she removes her shoes. Uncomfortable sensations of itchiness from her stockings mix with the sweat of the day. Sitting, she carefully removes her stockings, rubbing the dry skin around her ankles. As she reaches for some cream to apply to her skin, she thinks about what Greta told her.

**Her inner monologue takes over again:**
How dare that Melvin speak horribly about me! He knows my secret—how? I was discreet when I was courting the affluent man who paid the grocery clerk and paid my boarding fees. Owen leaving was devastating. Survival required food. How many people know? Surely, someone saw me with those men. I'll die with this secret. That government man has it written in his ledger. I must banish these thoughts. Madame Paumie rescued me.
Sena spent her summer days at the dye house and nights at the theater. She stashes saves change under the floorboards, as she often saw her mother do. She earned enough for work boots one week.

Exiting the theater Saturday night, Frank grabs her overcoat and hands it to Sena. As she slipped her arms into her overcoat, noticing a change in Frank's demeanor, she asks. "Are you okay?"

Frank pulling the door open for her, nods in somber silence not cracking jokes.

Gritty streets break the silence of there as they walk down the street.

Frank breaks the silence. "Come with me, Sena."

"What? Where?" Gasps Sena.

"There's a new opportunity for me in Missoula." Explains Frank.

Sena shakes her head, "I can't. My job is here. I am good at it."

Frank pressing her, "You were meant to entertain, Sena!"

"Nah, Frank, your job was to entertain with jokes and a carefree notions... What's it called again?" Sena asks.

"Wit?" Replies Frank winks.

Arriving at the edge of the Paumie block, Sena stares at the ground noticing the glittering speckles among the dirt, "I will miss you."

"Miss me? The jokester?" The moonlight casting upon them.

"Alright, promise you'll write?" Demands Frank.

"Promise."

# Let's Be Frank

Dear Reader,
You will notice there are multiple Franks in this book—6, to be exact. You have just met the first one, Frank S. Gates. All of them were real people, and their names remain unchanged. To keep things clear, I have done my best to use "Frank" in dialogue, but refer to them by their last names in narration.

FRANK S. GATES
Irish Comedian, Singer and Dancer, at the Airdome Tonight.

**Here is a quick guide to the Franks you'll encounter:**
- **Frank S. Gates**—Irish vaudeville comedian.
- **Franklin "Frank" J. Pierce**—owner of The Gem Theatre. Typically referred to as "Pierce" or "Frank."
- **Franklin J. Pierce, Jr.**—referred to as Frank, Jr.
- **Francis "Frank" Edwin Pierce** — Percy Prescott Pierce's son. No relation to the other Pierce family in Missoula.
- **Frank Lichti**—cigar maker in Missoula, Montana.
- **Frank B. Carroll**—vaudeville comedian.

A character glossary at the end of the book provides a list of each character, both historic and fictional. A brief biography of Franklin J. Pierce and his wife Mary is also featured. Now that you know who is who, I hope this helps you keep track of the Franks as the story unfolds!

# Chapter 3

**Summer 1900, Butte Montana**

S oft knocking rattles the door as Sena pins her hair. "Moment—Toe!" she calls, accentuating the end of the word in her quaint Swedish way. She places her hairbrush on the bed walks to answer the door.

"Oh, hi, Greta," she greets warmly.

Without waiting for an invitation, Greta steps assertively into Sena's apartment. For someone typically so shy, her abruptness startles Sena.

"We must talk at once," Greta blurts, pacing back and forth.

Sena watches her in confusion, her eyes catching the glint of sunlight on Greta's ornate floral hairpin. It was not cheap; the diamonds were genuine. A quiet inner voice questions how Greta could afford such luxury and why she had not sold it to escape her circumstances.

Suddenly, Greta stomps her foot, piercing Sena with a sharp

look. "Sena! Have you heard a word I have says?" she demands, frustration ringing in her tone.

"Sorry, go on," Sena replies, snapping back to attention.

"As I was saying, my husband Eben came to my door last night. He's back."

"Oh?" Sena's brows furrow. Unaware that Greta has a husband. "Is this not good news?"

"Heavens, no!" Greta exclaims. "That scoundrel drinks from daylight to dusk and raises his hands to me. Blackened and bloodied—that's what I've been. Last week, I visited an attorney about a divorce. Eben's been gone for nearly seven months! Now he's back, refusing to let me go."

"Oh, Greta," Sena murmurs, sympathy heavy in her voice.

"Will you come with me to the lawyer at noon?" Greta asks, clasping her hands tightly at her waist.

"Of course," Sena says, placing her hands over Greta's in reassurance. "But for now, I must go. Madame Paumie is expecting me."

At the dye house, Sena works to calculate textile measurements, place orders and select dyes, but her mind lingers on Greta's plight. Her nerves plainly visible, an hour into her work, Madame Paumie's hand startled her on the shoulder.

"Sena, ma chérie, what troubles you?" Madame Paumie asks, her French accent quick and concerned.

Sena jumps, taking a moment to catch her breath. She places her hands at the back of her neck, trying to ease the tension.

"Come now, discuss with me," Paumie urges, guiding Sena to a quieter corner.

Sena hesitates, but the urgency spills out. "It's Greta. Her husband returned after months of abandonment. He's hurt her before, and she's trying to divorce him. She asks me to go with her to the attorney at twelve-noon."

Madame Paumie's eyes widen. "Zis is serious, ma fille. We must help her. I will arrange it." She turns to an employee, issuing instructions to find Greta and relieve her for the day. Then, turning back to Sena, she adds, "We will go together. You both need support in zis matter."

At the attorney's office, Madame Paumie takes charge, commanding the room with confidence. Paumie guides Greta through legal questions, ensuring her voice was heard. Unexpectedly, Paumie turns toward Sena. "And you, ma petite, will you file papers against your missing husband?"

Sheer dread washes over Sena. Shaking her head, she whispers, "No. Surely Owen will return."

The attorney nods. "Very well," he says, addressing Greta. "Mrs. Clark, I need your signature here. I will notify you when you need to appear in court."

Greta signs on the line, her hands trembling slightly.

Weeks passed. When the court date arrives, Sena accompanies Greta. Eben did not show to contest the divorce, and the judge grants the decree. As they leave the courtroom, relief overcomes Greta. Tears streak her face as she and Sena walk side by side through the dusty streets. A light sprinkle of rain turns the dust into a thin layer of mud, clinging to their shoes and clothes. They hurry back to the dye house, laughing at their muddied state and the absurdity of it all.

The next day, they begin searching for a new apartment, because their wages allow them to dream of better accommodations. Every advertisement in the newspaper they find is beyond their means.

"Perhaps next week," Greta says optimistically, "the paper will have an advertisement for lodging fit for the likes of us."

A few weeks later, Greta learns of a meeting of divorced women and urges Sena to attend. Though hesitant, Sena agreed.
Sena hears Greta's typical knock on the door, looking in the mirror, she swipes of a finger across her tongue to wet down the flyways tending to her neat bun. She then gracefully opens the door and says, "Right, time to go?" Grabbing her overcoat and they proceed outside walking and looking up at the evening sky.

Walking side by side in stride, Greta, holding a pamphlet with the meeting address, led the way. Greta's pace was faster than hers because of her long legs and stature. Sena felt awkward trying to keep up the pace, yet her vertically challenged self feels defeat. She wonders what it was like to be tall and lanky. Sena constantly notices herself looking up frequently. Gaining perspective of what it's like to be tall? They approached a seemingly unmarked building as if it was vacant; it appears as though a former grocer has vacated the premises. Greta says, "Well, I believe this is the location."

"Are you certain?" Asks Sena.

Pointing down at the pamphlet, "This is the address, and it says enter the side door with the star on it. Be sure to knock twice before opening the door. There is a star on the door." Greta knocked twice. The door opens and a homely-looking woman looks both ways before she ushers them inside.

The woman says, "Down these stairs."

Sena and Greta walk down the rickety stairs, so narrow Sena

feels she might slip. Voices and the scent of strong coffee filled the basement. Around thirty women are gathered, their chatter ceasing as a poised woman spoke. Sena and Greta found a couple of empty chairs. The woman's lecture emphasized temperance, linking the destruction of marriages to the likes of liquor and vice. Sena zeroed in on the minuscule details of the lecturer—the woman's stature, intellect and ease speaking to the crowd. She admires the woman's courage yet found her repetitive use of the word "ye" and "the" utterly annoying. Then the woman makes a remark that resonates with Sena.

The lecturer raises her arm and points to many women in the room, her voice raises, "Ye shall NOT be compelled to shame for thine divorced state! Ye chose self-dignity over living in perpetual vulgarity."

The woman discusses the temperance movement and suffrage. Sena was uncertain what temperance means, yet she was well versed in suffrage from her experience in Helena.

After the lecture, Sena waits, drinking some coffee at the back while Greta chats with a few women. Greta seems to come out of her shell socializing. Sena is pleased to see Greta's reserved nature melting away. Sena does not feel social, anything but—she wants to hide away the emotional toll on her body after hearing about how she should not feel shame about divorce lingering in her future. It makes her stomach churn.

Greta's gaze met Sena's—and she senses Sena was feeling uneasy. Walking towards Sena, "Are you ready to leave?"

Sena nods.

As they climb the rickety staircase, the homely woman greets them once again.  She opens the door, peers into the alley, and then nods, allowing them to exit. Sena felt uneasy about this process. Due to the secrecy, Sena wonders if they are they doing something illegal? Sena is not aware of all the laws in America. In high school, she struggled with the government and citizenship classes. She cannot shake the feeling she might be doing something wrong.

As Greta and Sena stroll down the street into the night, they pass several men and couples who nod and tilt their hats. One man, who tilts his hat and lifts his cigar from his mouth, gives Sena an eerie feeling that makes her pick up her pace.

Greta, noticing Sena's faster pace and labored breathing, asks, "Are you quite alright?"

Sena continues running, huffing and puffing until the Paumie Block was in sight. Reaching the dye house apartments, she runs up the stairs ahead of Greta. Sena collapses at the top of the stairs and bursts into tears. Her sobbing steadily increases. Greta sits down on the top step, pulling out her handkerchief and wipes the tears away from Sena's cheeks and sweat upon her forehead.

They sat there in silence for several minutes. With each passing minute, Sena slowly regains her composure. Sena bites her lower lip, taking a deep breath, sighing, "I think I must. I must file papers."

Greta asks, "For a divorce?"

Sena with solemn sad eyes nods. Whispering, then raising the octave to a deep scream, "I can't!" repeatedly. Despair and raspiness from her sobbing state, "Owen was not a drunk. There was no ill treatment. He loves me, *He loves me!* He charmed me. He challenged me to be all that I could be. He is not like those other men. He is coming back. He is, Greta, do you hear me? He is coming ba—" the welling tears engulf her words.

Greta places her hands gently on Sena's shoulders, "Fret not. Shame not," then hands her a handkerchief to her to wipe away the tears. Greta continues, "He abandoned you. He deceived you." Sena somberly rises from the floor and walks to her room as Greta says, "Sena…you really must—file those papers."

## Excursion to Great Falls, Montana, Summer 1900

Scurrying around the apartment, Sena dresses in a traveling suit and her best hat. She only owns two traveling suits. It was the best one for a trip to another city. Greta has convinced Sena to take a trip to the Stockholm Theater in Great Falls. They are excited about this concert. They were told about the concert from Lulu who was always abreast of the best traveling acts because of her father's connections. There was to be a wonderful concert by the queen of soubrettes, Zeta Lovell. The newspapers report her voice to be exquisite. Sena sings under her breath, humming along throughout, picking up things and dropping them into her travel case.

When they arrive at the Butte depot, the sun's rays are beaming as they wait upon the platform. Time elapses. Ten minutes feels more like an hour. As the passengers await the train, they are eager to board. Being there, she is reminded of her arrival in Montana as a teenager and meeting Martin Holter. She wishes she could slink back into time, making different choices. Her stomach has a gnawing ache for Owen's return. She wishes the shame would melt away. She wishes to be a dignified woman with her husband intact. In the distance, she heard the steam whistle and the train's axles churning on the metal cogs.

As they moved closer to the train, an elderly woman fanning herself inquired haughtily, "Are you two young women unchaperoned by a male?"

Greta pipes up, "Why yes, we are, we are working women," then pushed past her. Sena follows suit. Greta looks over her shoulder, shooting a sly grin to Sena as they shuffles towards their seat. They engage in a hearty laugh.

Sena sighs, "Well, are we not hoity-toity? Is that what it's called?"

Greta nods, emphasizing her thick British accent, "Indeed, we are not any such of the sort."

Upon their arrival in Great Falls, they secure accommodations at the Milwaukee Hotel. To Sena's surprise, she sees a man she recognizes at the bar. A large muscular man who resembles a teddy bear. It was Curly who had worked at Christie's Saloon in Butte. As it would be wildly inappropriate for her to swagger up to the bar to say hello; she peeks from the hallway into the bar. She walks back and forth, fanning herself hoping he will look her way and notice her.

At last, he sees her, nods, wipes a glass and leaves the empty bar to the fuller lobby.

"Well, hello Miss Sena, what brings you to Great Falls?" Says Curly with a baritone charismatic ring.

Sena bows her head and looks up, "My friend Greta and I have come to see a show at the Stockholm."

"Nice to meet you, Greta." Curly turns toward Sena, "Are you still performing? How is your mother?" He asked.

"Mother has gone on to San Francisco. No, I am working at the Paumie Dye House." Sena says with confidence.

"Taking orders," Greta adds, "In the office."

"Oh," Curly lets out a slight chuckle, "Well, enjoy your time in Great Falls."

They all nod farewell. Sena and Greta find their way to their hotel room. They rest before attending the show.

They find their way to their seats in the Stockholm theater. A full crowd anticipates Zeta Lovell to come onstage to dazzle them with her voice.

While Miss Lovell's voice is exquisite, the comical words of Miss Anna DeKoven's performance prompts them to laugh with great ease. The reverberating laughter relaxes their muscles and tension built up from working daily. Carefree notions sweep across their bodies making them feel much lighter—heavy burdens cast away like shedding skin. They find all the acts fabulous including the twins. The Kennison Sisters, who show off their acrobatic feats.

After the show, as they exit the theater, they promenade down the street. They notice women entering a side door. They curiously glance at one another. Sena and Greta exchange a glance, silently agreeing to check it out. Their adventurous side leaps toward the door—reaching the door as it closes on them. Sena grins as she places her hand upon the doorknob. Entering, they soon realize it is a private party, with men and women holding glasses filled to the brim—it is definitely NOT a temperance event. They continue to mingle through the crowd, blending in as if they belong at the party.

Greta laughingly whispers to Sena, "I quite think we are *not* supposed to be here."

Sena smiles and weaves over to the table set with delicious hors d'oeuvres and drinks. Sena reaches for a petite cake, as she looks up she meet Curly's eyes. Her eyes widen.

Curly laughs, "Sena, were you invited to this gathering?"

Sena grins, mouth full of food, she covers her mouth, shaking her head no.

"Well, go on, have a delight. Secret is safe here."

As they mingle through the crowd, she accidentally bumps into someone—as she spins around she says, "I apologi—"

Sena sees it is Anna DeKoven, the comedienne from the

Stockholm Theatre.

Anna tells jokes to others gathered around her; she remains unphased by Sena bumping into her. Sena notices Anna chatting with a circle of lively and laughing actresses, including the Kennison twins. The women act with a carefree nature.

Bravely, Sena speaks up, "I'm Sena."

Jessie Kennison asks. "Oh, like Lean-a? with a *Sin* to it, eh?"

Sena laughs, with them. She is unsure if they were poking fun at her or not. She continues to engage in an enjoyable chat with the women.

Anna says, "Sena dear, you must come to my wedding in Missoula," then points to the Kennison Sisters, "Daisy and Jessie will be there as well."

Daisy Kennison claps enthusiastically repeatedly says, "Yes!" She continues extending her hands to Sena, "You really must come, it will be simply a grand time!"

# Chapter 4

**1901, Butte, Montana**

Upon Sena and Greta's return to Butte, Sena had a postcard from Marie Sanderlin in Helena.

"Who is Marie? Asks Greta.

"I lived with her family in Helena while I was attending high school." Sena looking down at the postcard smiling. "Isn't it grand you can send these cards now in the mail? Brief notes."

Sena and Greta begin unpacking their travel cases.

Marie's postcard asks Sena to visit Helena for an acrobatic performance at the Broadwater Park in Helena.

"Oh, that sounds exciting!" Says Marie.

"Yes," Sena responds without emotion and skipping subjects, "Hmmm, I suppose its time." Sena says placing a brush on her dressing table.

"Time for...? Greta asks.

"Filing for the divorce." Sena looks somber.

In the weeks that follow, Sena takes the necessary steps to dissolve her brief marriage to Owen Bockley, the vaudeville comedian who had abandoned her after just eleven days. To take her mind off the shame cast upon her filing for divorce, she and several others journey to Helena to watch the acrobatic show. As she watches the Samayoas stretching their bodies and contorting in unexplainable ways, her feelings mirror their stretches. Torn yet stronger. She finds herself admiring Manuel Samayoa's lean muscular body and the envy she had of his wife Cleo who could dance effortlessly. Her envious thoughts quickly turn to lust. The way his tight costume wraps around his legs. She finds herself wanting him more and more, yet realizes fully this is an unattainable notion. She wonders if her thoughts are normal. She has no one she feels comfortable to confide in nor to confer with about these newfound arousals.

Back in Butte, Sena walks down the street toward the mercantile for sundries. She startles as she hears a man say, "Must have been a hag," as he passes her by.

Her body tenses. Heat rises upon her cheeks. A paperboy dashes towards her, waving his the latest edition near her face

"Paper, miss?" the paperboy enthusiastically shouts.

Wordlessly, she hands over a coin, unfolding the pages with trembling fingers. And there it is, bold as brass:

> THE GREAT OWEN BOCKLEY DESERTS WIFE AFTER 11 DAYS.
> WIFE SEEKS DIVORCE AND FORMER NAME REINSTATED.

A sickening wave of humiliation crashes over her. Her stomach twists in knots. Her blood boiling in her veins. Her name—intimate details of her life—splashed across the pages for all to gawk. She storms toward her lawyer's office, her grip tightening around the crumpled paper.

Inside, a clerk barely has time to react as Sena storms in with fury. "Miss, wait—Attorney Carroll is with a client, you can't—"

Ignoring the clerk, Sena stomps quickly through the office space, slamming the crumpled paper onto the attorney's desk. "It was a private matter!" She seethes, punctuating her words with a string of Swedish curse words.

Attorney Carroll leans back in his chair, unimpressed by her outburst. "Now, Miss Bjork. A legal matter such as this is public record. The newsmen loiter around the courtrooms for stories to print. I could not have prevented this."

Swallowing hard, she turns to leave, forcing her feet to carry her to the one place where she could work to forget about this situation—Paumie's Dye House. Walking, she remains in a hazy state of confusion. As she walks through the streets she becomes emotional as she hears snippets of whispers. The sideways glances she receives feels like a heavy blanket of judgment pressing down on her psyche. The whispers. The stares. People delighting in her suffering as entertaining gossip.

Entering the dye house, the weight of eyes upon her makes her stomach queasy. She feels as though she is in a glass case, on display for all of Butte to sneer.

Madame Paumie, ever perceptive, steps with precision into the center of the dye house floor. "Does anyone have words to say?" Her sharp eyes scan the workers. "Non?" She claps her hands. "Back to work, oui or non? Tres bien."

The room buzzes back to life, yet Sena sees others continue to murmur.

The remaining court proceedings are brief. Owen's absence seals the judge's decision. She legally restores her maiden name—Sena Bjork. A fresh start.

Sena and Greta find a modest apartment together, two newly divorcees navigating a world that offers little grace for those in their situation. Society's judgment is harsh, they bear its weight quietly, masking their shame while striving to carve out a future on their own terms.

Their first night in their new apartment, Sena dips her pen into the inkwell and began a letter.

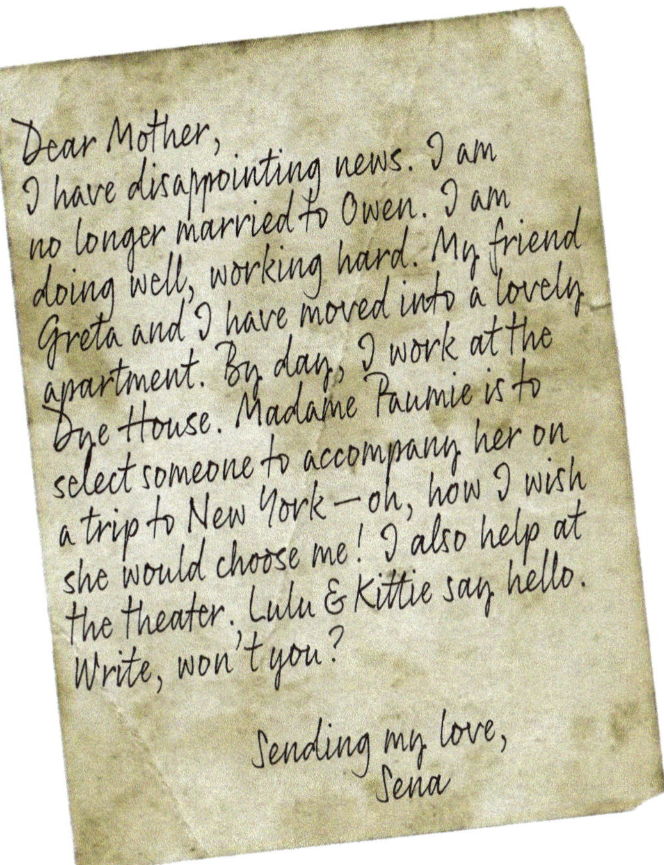



Madame Paumie's upcoming trip to New York stirs anticipation among the employees. This opportunity to study the finest new styles and fabrics is rare. Sena years for this chance. One of many vying for the opportunity.

A new hire at the Dye House, Esmie, had made sure of that. From the moment she arrived, she seemed determined to upstage Sena in every way.

One afternoon, Sena finds Esmie inspecting a delicate order—a silk gown belonging to one of Butte's wealthiest patrons.

"That's already been mixed," Sena says, noting the dye Esmie was preparing.

Esmie barely glances up. "I prefer my method."

Sena's jaw tightened. "But Madame Paumie gave specific instructions—"

"Maybe you misheard her." Esmie gives a saccharine smile before tilting the dye vat.

Sena's sharp rebuttal bites back with frustration. When the gown emerges streaked and blotchy, Esmie disappears conveniently before Madame Paumie can see the disaster. Sena stays late, fixing Esmie's mistakes.

By the time Sena makes it to the theater, she is breathless—and then she sees, who? Esmie! Onstage! In her spot!

"John!" Sena hisses at the stage manager. "What is she doing up there?"

John barely looks at her. "You were not here. We needed a voice."

Sena fumes. "So I'm demoted to chorus girl?"

"Tonight, you're in the dance number. Learn fast." John says.

Cursing under her breath, Sena spends the night rehearsing new difficult choreography. By the time she reaches her bed, her body aches, barely registering Greta's snore in the room. The next morning, she awakes realizing she overslept. Sena begins to panic. She rushes to ready herself for the day. She rushes to the Dye House, breathless as she enters. Madame Paumie signals for her to step into the office. Esmie is already there.

"Sena," Madame Paumie says, hands folded. "It has come to my attention that you made errors on this account."

Sena stiffens. "I—"

Madame Paumie held up a hand. "Thankfully, Esmie corrected them. And you are late this morning. Let's not have this lackadaisical nature."

Sena balls her hands into fists. Esmie smirks. As they exit the office, Sena leans in, whispering, "Why are you trying to destroy me?"

Esmie eyes widen, feigning innocence. "Whatever do you mean?" She strolls away without another glance.

Sena marches to Greta's side, voice low. "Why did you not wake me?"

Greta, working with the dyes, whispers back, "I thought you might have the day off."

Months pass, with Sena pushing herself harder and harder. The rivalry with Esmie grows fiercer by the day. Sena refuses to let her win.

Not at the Dye House.

Not at the theater.

And certainly not in life.

# Chapter 5

**November 1901, Butte, Montana**

Strolling down the street, Sena approaches the post office counter, she asks the clerk, "Sena Bjork, any post for me today?"

The clerk nods and turns to fetch the mail. "Looks as though we have a multiple for you today."

Sena excitedly flips through the stack of postal letters, and fills with disappoint as there is no word from her mother.

Sena's heart bubbles with excitement. The Kennison twins' invite to spend Christmas with them in Deadwood, South Dakota. Their mutual friend, Anna DeKoven's wedding in Missoula. Sena finds it splendid to have two invitations to events, month after month. All the exciting travel possibilities flickering in her mindscape during her walk to the dye house. Stepping inside, she picks up a paper sack; quickly she jots down the math—train fare, hotel, food. Her looming attorney's fees worry her. If her figures are accurate, surely she has the funds to travel on a vacation. She wonders—
"Would Madame Paumie allow this absence?"

Walking through the dye house, she searches for Madame Paumie. Passing an employee, she says, "Have you seen Madame Paumie? The employee points towards the back room. She continues her search. Upon reaching the door frame of the back room—in view, she saw Madame Paumie is making adjustments to a dress form. "Madame, may I have a word?"

Madame Paumie glances up. "What is it, chérie?"

Hesitating, Sena timidly speaks, "I'd like to take leave. A month's travel to visit Deadwood and Missoula."

Madame Paumie smiled and nods. "You have earned it. Take your time, Sena."

Relief washes over her. "Thank you, Madame Paumie."

Loud sounds and screams came from another part of the dye house. Madame Paumie and Sena exchange an alarming glance and run towards the commotion.

Esmie stands covered head to toe in blue dye. Everyone's eyes are wide in disbelief.

Sena and Greta exchange a glance, both trying to contain sly grins as Esmie had this coming, taking shortcuts and rushing.

"What happened here?" Asks Madame Paumie.
"I... had a little accident." Esmie cries.

"A little accident?" Madame Paumie questioned. "You're blue from head to toe!"

Sena tries to hold back laughter. "Maybe next time don't rush things, Esmie."

Pulling out her suitcase, Sena's blood bubbles with excitement, yet very glance over at Greta left her sad. She wishes Greta could accompany her.

"Greta, I wish you could come with me," Sena says softly.

Greta looked down at the linens she was folding, avoiding eye contact. "Go on now, don't worry about me."

Sena opens the jar.  She reaches inside and grabs some bills. She places the bills on Greta's nightstand. She says, "Here's for January's rent," she said.

Greta nods and looks noticeably sad.

Continuing to pack, Sena's mind wanders to her nemesis, Esmie. She hopes she does not cause problems while she is gone.

The next morning, Sena rises early to catch the train. She tiptoes lightly, careful to not wake Greta. Sena looks at her reflection in the mirror. She wets her fingers and slicks back the flyaways in her bun. Before she exits, she casts her gaze upon the small apartment.

## Christmas, 1901, Deadwood, South Dakota

Deadwood bustles with excitement. The Eagles Benefit is a grand affair, filling the Opera House with eager spectators. Barrel jumpers, acrobats and singers grace the stage, while the Kennison Sisters twist their bodies in contrary ways. Audience members squirm in amazement.

As a man takes the stage and sings barritone the lyrics of *Old Jim's Christmas Hymn*, a dashing man in the audience distracts Sena. She is mesmerized by his grin. She tries to focus her attention to the man singing on stage, yet her eyes fixate on the dashing man in the audience. Beside him is an older woman who bears a striking resemblance to him. Their eyes meet exchanging flirtatious glances. He nods and grins, causing her cheeks to flush a berry tone. They turn their heads occasionally, acting as though the entertainment is their focal point. Sena sees moving pictures for the first time. The theater shows *Little Red Riding Hood*. It was she sits transfixed, absorbing the flickering images. As the final scene fades, she feels a pang of disappointment—wishing she could watch it again, to linger in its magic a little longer.

**Old Jim's Christmas Hymn**
Through the snow, so pure and bright,
Shines a candle's gentle light.
Voices lifted, sweet and true,
Sing of Christmas, old and new.
Gather close, both friend and kin,
Let the Christmas joy begin.
Blessings round the fire's glow,
Peace and love 'mid winter's snow.
--William B. Gray, 1896

After the benefit, Sena spent a joyful Christmas with the Kennison Sisters before heading on to Missoula for Anna DeKoven's wedding.

## January 1902, Train Ride to Montana

On the train ride from Deadwood, South Dakota to Missoula, Montana the rhythmic clacking of the wheels on the tracks filled the air. Daisy and Jessie were both peacefully asleep, their soft breaths blending with the gentle hum of the train. Sena, lost in thought, cannot shake the image of the man from the Eagles' benefit. She could still recall the faint scent of his cologne, a mix of musk and cedarwood that she got a whiff of as she exited the theater. His sandy brown hair, with strands of blonde catching the glow of the gaslit lamps, framed his symmetrical face. The memory of his piercing gaze lingers in her mind, making her heart race. A fleeting encounter with a dashing stranger, a moment suspended in time as the train journeys on.

As Sena's mind wanders back to the encounter over and over again, her heart quickens its pace, sending a rush of adrenaline through her veins. The physical effects of her swirling emotions create a tingling sensation spreading from her chest to her fingertips. Her palms become clammy, a reaction to the mix of excitement and uncertainty that clouded her thoughts.

As the train nears Missoula, Sena finds herself caught in a whirlwind of emotions. Her breathing becomes shallower, the rhythmic rise and fall of her chest mirroring the cadence of the train. A knot forms in her stomach tugging at her insides. She reaches for a piece of candy to soothe her.

As Sena steps off the train in Missoula, she notices the light hits differently in this new city, casting everything in a golden glow. The familiar landscapes take on a new charm. A deep sense of renewal washes over her. Exhilarating shivers run through her, not from the cold, but from a strange, premonition. It feels as though the universe is whispering secrets of great things to come. Missoula, with its picturesque surroundings and welcoming atmosphere. With anticipation in her heart, she takes a deep breath, ready to embrace whatever adventure lies ahead.

# Chapter 6

**January 1902, Missoula, Montana**

Frigid winds made the journey uncomfortable. Sena, and the Kennison twins—Daisy and Jessie secured a carriage upon arriving at the depot. They came to attend Anna DeKoven's wedding. Wherever they traveled, the Kennison sisters always found performance opportunities. Entertainers received lodging at The Gem Theatre.

There was a distinct heaviness felt by the layers of clothing upon their cold skin. Even the carriage robe upon their laps could not deter the chill in the air as they rode over to The Gem Theatre.

A tall older gentleman greeted them at the door, "Welcome, Davenport is the name. Most call me Davy. And you must be the Kennison twins—resemblance remarkable. Pierce has spoken fondly of you—says you two put on a class-act."

Daisy laughs, "Yes, and this is our friend, Sena. She has accompanied us to attend Anna's wedding."

Davenport stately response. "Very well, your rooms are on the third floor. Allow me to get the keys.'"

As the Kennison twins and Davenport engage in polite chitchat, Sena's is captivated by the grandeur of the theater. It takes over her senses—as the cold air dissipates, the subtle fragrances of tobacco, coconut and pine made for a cozy environment. A long bar along the side frames the room with a rounded archway leading to the orchestra area and stage. Scattered small tables and straight back chairs filled the large room. The stage looks magical with warm glows of the gaslight lamps lining the room. Sena notices as a man is tinkering in the orchestra area.

Davenport signals in military fashion to the man tinkering, "Dave, will you show these ladies to their quarters?"

Popping up from crouching, the stage illuminated, "A ha! Got it to work!" Then looking their way smiles, "Sure, right this way ladies." Daisy is curious and asks Dave Kelsey a lot of questions about his tinkering. She learns he is the electrician for the nightly show. He is responsible for the mechanics to illuminate the stage.

After settling into her room, Sena wanders through the theater, eager to take in its beauty.

Descending onto the second floor, there was a small bar. Sena brushes her hand across the bar top feeling its smooth surface as she inspects about a dozen private booths with a balcony view of the stage. The paisley drapes pulled to each side make the small table look exclusive. At the last booth, she picks up a piece of paper. It is a playbill from a past show. She notices a headline that reads, "Rules." She thinks, *"Rules?"*

**Reading on:**
*Performers playing in this house must bear in mind that they are playing to an intelligent audience and that any old thing' don't go. Vulgar or profane language, cigarette smoking or any actions unbecoming a lady will subject the offender to immediate dismissal. The Gem Concert Hall is devoted to drama, burlesque and high-class vaudeville.*

She continues to read the playbill, a familiar voice echoes from the stage below. A wide smile spreads across her face as she recognizes the voice—Frank Gates, the Irish comedian from Butte. She quickly steps toward the balcony. Leaning over she sees Frank rehearsing mid-joke, delivering one of his signature Irish quips. Sena bursts into laughter and claps her hands in delight. He pauses and looks up as a grin splits across his face.

"Aye, Sena!" Frank Gates waves.

"Comical as ever, Frank!" Exclaims Sena.

"What brings you to Missoula?" Frank Gates asks, shading his eyes against the stage lights.

"Anna DeKoven's wedding. Traveled here with the Kennison sisters."

"Aye, I'll be at the wedding as well. We are all meeting out front to load up and head over to Frank Lichti's home for the festivities," Frank Gates says as he wipes his brow theatrically.

Sena smiles, waves goodbye and walks up to the 3rd floor.  In her room, she carefully braids her hair into a crown around her bun. Focused thoughts on the wedding lead her to ponder if she will ever marry again.  She yearns for a real wedding—one with a minister, a proper dress, flowers and guests. A knock at her door interrupts her thoughts. Jessie pops her head in, more chipper than usual, "Coming?"

Yes... Sena stands, wrapping her scarf around her neck and pulling on her overcoat. Stopping to look in the mirror she licks her finger and slicks back a small flyaway near her ear.

Outside, a group of guests gathered around a wagon lined with hay bales. They all loaded up, snuggling under lap robes to keep warm during their short travel.

A sharply dressed man with a jolly demeanor made his way around to the back—the sound of his golden cane hitting the gravel. Checking on everyone, "All good back here?" He asks, his eyes landing on Sena. "Do we have a new resident?"

Daisy pipes up, "Yes, she's with us—gonna go to Anna's wedding."

The gentleman nods, holding onto his derby hat so it doesn't fly away and fidgeting with his cane, giving Sena a warm smile. "And does the lovely lady have a name?"

"Sena," she answers, returning the smile.

Pierce nods warmly at Sena. "Why—lovely to meet you, Miss Sena. Welcome. I'm Mr. Pierce—I own this entertainment place. Isn't it a gem?" Then, addressing the group, he calls, "Okay, let's gooo!" Have some fun elongating the last word with a playful o.

As the wagon trundles along, laughter and song fill the crisp evening air. Jessie, clearly a few drinks in, sways slightly as she leans toward Sena.

Jessie takes a swig from her flask. "Anna marrying George? I don't get it," she mumbles slurring her words. "He's in charge of a saloon—"

A hand reaches out and plucks the flask from Jessie's grasp.

"Give that back!" Jessie whines.

"You've had enough," says an overly handsome and rugged man with thick black hair. He says it firmly, his voice brooking no argument.

Daisy hushes her sister by patting her on the shoulder. "Jessie, shhh! Let's not ruin Anna's day."

Jessie grumbled and whined under her breath.

Frank Gates lightheartedly chimes in, "Anna is a grown lass— she can take care of herself. If you ask me, it's likely a business arrangement." He turns toward Sena and points to the good-looking man with black hair, "Have you met Spider?"

Sena blushes shaking her head no.

*Even decades after the theater closed and Spider was gone, Missoulians reminisced that he had an uncanny resemblance to 1930s movie star Clark Gable.*

Frank continues, "Well, this is Spider, he bartends at The Gem. He's quite accustomed to knowing when drinkers have reached all they can consume. And when to keep on servin'." Frank Gates winks, "And, this is Sena. She's my friend from the Butte circuit."

Spider nods. His nod is rhythmic with the bumps from the wheel of the wagon. Sena uncontrollably blushes and looks away to avoid awkward eye contact. She gazes toward mountains in the distance, their snow-capped peaks glow in the evening sky.

Upon arrival, Sena admires the grand Victorian home with its wraparound porch. As the guests disembark, the men chat about the cigars they hope to sample. The host, Frank Lichti, is a local cigar maker.

Daisy leans in close to Sena, "Help me with my sister. Keep her upright, will you?"

Spider interjects, "I'll assist you with getting her into the house," he gentlemanly locks his arm in hers on one side, Daisy on the other, both guiding Jessie to the door.

Once inside, Sena took Spider's place, with Daisy, they guided Jessie toward a table where petite sandwiches and cucumber slices were arranged. Sena scans the room, spotting a woman watching her with kind eyes.

"Here, let's get her some coffee," the woman offered. "Mary Pierce. And you are?"

"Sena."

"A guest of the bride, I presume?" Mary asks as she pours the coffee.

"Yes. I met Anna in Great Falls at a performance."

"She's a fine performer, isn't she? It's always grand when people can be entertained." Mary smiles warmly. "Here, this should help." She handed the coffee to Sena, who quickly passes it to Jessie. A bell rang, drawing the room's attention. Mr. Pierce stands at the center, tapping a triangular metal piece. Mary slightly chuckles placing a hand upon her heart. "Ah, my husband is about to charm us all."

Mr. Pierce raises his glass. "Friends, we gather here to celebrate George and Anna. Before they enter matrimony, let us wish them many happy years. Raise your glasses!"

Sena takes her spot to sing a song for the wedding. As she begins to sing, her heart races. The combination of nervousness and flattery creates a mix of excitement and apprehension. The heat of the room seemed to intensify, making her skin flush with a rosy hue. Her hands tremble slightly. The physical manifestation of her emotions are evident in her body language.

As she finished her last note, the weight of Mr. and Mrs. Pierce's gaze bore down on her, their whispered conversation adding to the tension in the air. Sena's stomach twisted in knots, her breath coming in shallow gasps as she tried to decipher their expressions. The uncertainty of their thoughts left her feeling vulnerable and exposed, her body reacting to the emotional rollercoaster she was experiencing.

Despite the physical effects of her emotions, Sena maintained her composure, a small smile on her lips as she curtsied and made her way back to her seat. The adrenaline coursing through her veins leave her feeling both drained and exhilarated, the intensity of the moment etched into her memory.

As the guests mingled, Sena chatted with Curly until the men went to another parlor to smoke cigars. Then she chatted with Anna, Mary and Mrs. Frank Lichti—Emma.

Sena became enthralled as Mary spoke of an extensive acting career. Listening attentively to Mary's stories of dawning stages in large cities like Chicago. Wails from the basket in the corner interrupted, turning their attention to the Pierce's baby Missoula. Mary gracefully glided across the floor to pick her up, "It's all right, Missy. It's all right," rocking her snugly in her arms. A southern smoothness in her dialect. Mary glancing at Emma as she swayed, "you'll soon be in the same boat as me."

Sighing Emma looking down and caressing her rounded stomach, "Yes, soon. I'm not entirely certain I will be as graceful as you caring for a babe."

"Nonsense, you'll be magnificent," Mary chimes.

Sena notices Jessie across the room. Jessie looks as though she is gaining her sobriety. Sena walks to the food table. She reaches for a cucumber sandwich. Frank Pierce approaches, leaning on his cane. He tilts his head. "Your voice is exquisite," he says. "I'd be delighted if you would sing at The Gem later this week." He smiles eagerly.

Sena feeling put on the spot grins in surprise.

Frank Pierce pressing her for an answer, "Please agree to this. The great people of Missoula shall be so lucky to hear a voice like yours."

Mary Pierce walks over to Sena with a baby on her hip and locks her arm in her husbands. "Oh, have you asks her?" The Pierce's were a united front.

Frank Pierce smiles wide, "Why yes."

Mary chimes in, "Please, say yes."

Sena chews on her cucumber and raising her hand to cover her mouth, after swallowing, "Okay."

"Grand! —I'll add you to the lineup." Pierce's magnetic charm was contagious. He let go of Mary's arm, looked into his baby's eyes smiling, then spread his arms wide lifting his cane straight up into the air. "Marvelous! We shall dress you as a Swedish Nightingale gracing our stage!" Putting his cane down and leaning in, "You are Swedish, correct?"

Sena laughs slightly, "Yes."

"Grand! It will be great all 'round! The Frank's – Frank Gates and Carroll, The Kennison twins, you and more! Some of the greatest performers in America!" Frank Pierce speaks boastfully.

Shortly, thereafter, when it was time to leave. Frank Lichti being a gracious host gave out cigar boxes to every man who attended and handkerchiefs to all the ladies as they exited their home. Spider swaying back and forth almost as if he might burst into a jig as Frank Lichti hands him a box of cigars.

Sena notices Hartwell, the son of Frank Pierce, who she thought was about 10 yeas old was eager to get a box of cigars as well as the other men. She found it comical.

Hartwell's eyes lit up as he held the box firmly. There was an extra spring in his step. ""Thank ya kindly, sir."

The Mr. Lichti and Mr. Pierce exchange glances. Frank Pierce winks at his son, "Hartwell, you can take them--save them for a rainy day when you are older. "

As they walk to the carriages, Sena listens to Hartwell's Irish accent. She finds it interesting as his parents sound so much different.

The group from The Gem trudges back toward the wagon and piles in. The prickling of hay mixed with the cold air near her slightly exposed wrist, where her glove is a bit short feels like an uncomfortable sting. Once they all huddle in sharing the lap robe, the warmth becomes comforting. Yawning, Sena's eyes water, her head bobbles down toward Gates' shoulder, and she drifts to sleep with the rhythm of the wagon wheels.

The wheels screech to a halt at the entrance of The Gem. Daisy walks alongside Spider and Frank Gates, who help carry Sena up to her room and lay her upon her bed. She does not wake. Spider whispers, "here," grabbing an extra blanket from a drawer and handing it to Daisy. The men exit. Daisy gently removes Sena's shoes and places a blanket upon her.  "Night, sweet girl."

## Wedding, January 12, 1902, Missoula, Montana

Anna Hoefer's, (stage name Anna DeKoven) wedding to George Nink, proprietor of The Louvre, 117 N. Higgins in Missoula. The wedding took place at the home of Frank and Emma Lichti, who resided at 1214 Toole Avenue on the west side of Missoula. The wedding was officiated by Rev. F. J. Salsman of the Emmanuel Baptist Church in Missoula, Montana. The newly married couple, Mr. and Mrs. George Nink honeymooned in Spokane, Washington.

Fictional dialogue and situational analysis has been added to the this event for the book's narrative.

# Chapter 7

**January 27, 1902, Missoula, Montana**

Nervous flutters hit Sena's stomach a few hours before her performance when Gates knocked. "Are you all set?"

"Ja—Yes," Sena says, her voice muffled through the door. She stuck a pin in her hair and glided out of her dressing chair to open the door.

Gates studied her and blurts, "Well, lass, your face looks contrary." "The people here are so genuine and kind; I'm really connecting with them," says Sena, a hint of contentment in her tone.

"C'mon," Gates chuckles, his eyes crinkling at the corners, "I'll walk you to the backstage dressing rooms; it's a bit of a maze back there."

"Fool, no laughing matter. I have to return to my employment in Butte," says Sena, trailing down the steps after Gates.

"Sounds like you've got a predicament," Gates says. "Bet that employment doesn't have dazzling Oriental dancers or fun jokesters like m'self."

Backstage swirled with the quiet energy of performers. Pierce and Davenport entered from the back, Davenport clapping to gather attention as Pierce took the floor, delivering a rousing pep talk. Pierce then dashed through the stage curtain to welcome guests to the show.

Hidden in the wings, Sena watches, captivated by the swirling silks and glittering jewelry of the Oriental dancers as they filled the stage with vibrant energy and the sounds of exotic music. Gates and Clarke's comedic routine was a riot of witty banter and slapstick, punctuated by the audience's uproarious laughter. Peeking through the wings, Sena's nerves were high. She wiggled her toes as Mr. Pierce walked toward the stage. Secretly, she wishes Owen was by her side. His smile to reassure her. His words of encouragement echoing in her mind. As she stands in the wings, she feels gut punched from his absence, yet heart sick for his presence. She kept glancing around, half-expecting him to appear out of nowhere. Despite her better judgment, she can't help but imagine him returning, a silly notion that tugged at her heart.

Sena caught whiffs of old wood and velvet in the air. The spotlight glinted off Mr. Pierce's derby hat as he moved with grace to center stage. The sound of his golden cane tapping on the stage echoed. She admired his skill to command an audience and make them feel like they were home in the theater.  When he spoke, she knew it was her cue to step on stage, "Folks, tonight we have an exquisite treat—the lovely Miss Sena, our Swedish Nightingale, will perform traditional Swedish songs!"

The applause swells as Sena took the stage.

After her performance, Frank Pierce approached her once more. "Stay in Missoula. I'll pay you a handsome sum—I assure you it will be worth staying."

The offer was tempting.

Later that night, chilly drafts swept past her exposed leg, stirring her from sleep. The covers had slipped away, leaving her skin vulnerable to the night air. She lay still, staring at the wooden slats of the floor, the dim light casting faint shadows across them. Time stretched endlessly as she willed herself back to sleep.

She wiggles her toes—a habit as familiar as breathing—then reached for the covers, tugging them back over herself. But her focus drifted to a particular floorboard, its dark rings forming a shape that resembled an apple. She traced them with her eyes, counting each one. The act stirred her hunger, and soon after, another urge followed.

With a sigh, she reached beneath the bed for the chamber pot, pushed aside the blanket, and squatted down. The steady trickle of urine echoed through the quiet room, and she tensed, worried it might wake the twins sleeping in the next room. But surely, they were fast asleep.

Minutes blurred into hours, and when sleep would not return, she surrendered to the wakefulness. There was no sense in lying there any longer.

Striking a match, she ignites the candle, its soft glow casting dancing shadows on the worn wooden table. The faint scent of geraniums filled the air as she rummages through her satchel. The sound of rustling paper echoing in the quiet room. Finding a piece of paper, she ran her fingers over its rough texture before picking up her pen to write to Greta. Lost in thought, she absentmindedly wiggles her toes, the familiar nervous habit bringing her a sense of comfort in the solitude. Alone in the dimly lit room, she has no one to talk to or share her thoughts with.

**Her inner monologue took over:**
Should I stay here in Missoula? I truly like the idea of singing in front of a crowd. The applause is quite a nice feeling. But – I feel important at the Dye House and Madame Paumie has been ever so generous to me. I wonder if she will be filled with anger. If she

will be quite upset with me after allowing me the time off. I would utterly hate to disappoint her. I feel like this community of people is lovely. Missoula seems nicer than Butte, with more beautiful elements, greenery. Heard someone say it is a "garden city." Much different from the grit of Butte. I don't mind Butte—it has charm, too, if one looks for it. If I was here and not there, perhaps I could escape the reality of being a shamed woman. A divorced woman. It is embarrassing to be a woman of my status. Here, I could have the clean slate. A new beginning. A new me. What about Greta? Should I write her and tell her to come to Missoula? Yes, but what shall she do to earn a living? Surely, there are already seamstresses here. Dare they have another? Greta would not enjoy the entertainment life.

**She took out a pencil to write to Greta:**

Dear Greta,

Missoula is a lovely city. I have resolved to stay in this place as I have been offered a lead role in entertaining at The Gem Theatre. I am enclosing my extra portion for the coming months rent. I will continue to send you money until you secure a new roommate. Should you want to leave Butte—Missoula is a lovely city, alright. I hope Mme Paumie is not angry with me. I will write to her with my resignation.

Love, Sena

## February 1902, Missoula, Montana

The newspaper headline, "Chinese New Year Will Begin Today at 2' o'clock," Daisy read aloud as she relaxes on a tufted chaise lounge. Daisy looks up and exclaims, "Oh, this will be a dandy of fun!" Animated she continues reading aloud, "So complete Missoula celestials that represent their celebration this year be, and equally desirous of avoiding accident and trouble, they wish it announced that the racket begins at 2' o'clock this afternoon and a little caution with skittish horses would be advisable."  Daisy giggles, "This sounds like fun."

Jessie yawning, "What time is it?"

Daisy continues excitedly, "I've never celebrated Chinese New Year before! And it's not just one day—it lasts several days."

Sena offers a faint smile, not quite following the conversation. "It's nearly two in the afternoon." Sena thought to herself, one drawback about show business: late nights.

Suddenly, a loud crash and horses neighing and hooves clamoring interrupts their laughter. Sena and Daisy exchange alarmed glances. Without hesitation, Daisy grabs Sena's hand and pulls her towards the door. Time seems to slow as they sprint down the hallway towards the stairs. Just as they reach the bottom step, the back door swings open. Spider carrying a full load of spirits. The girls burst into laughter and sit upon the stairs.

"What has you girls in jolly spirits today?" Asks Spider.

"Wondering what all the commotion is outside." Daisy says, recovering from her intense laughter.

"Ah, it's the Chinese New Year celebration today. That's all." Spider says putting away the spirits. "Lots of fun fire poppers. Makes the horses skittish."

Once they had readied themselves for the day, they wandered into Missoula's small but lively Chinese district along Main Street. The scent of roast duck and five-spice drift from a restaurant on Front Street, mingling with the earthy aroma of dried herbs spilling from the open doors of a dry goods store. Red paper lanterns flutter in the cold breeze, and gold banners with intricate calligraphy hung above shop entrances, marking the celebration.

As they stroll, a Chinese man on a bicycle slowed as he approached them. It was John Quong, a Chinese merchant. He extended a black silk bag toward Sena, his expression warm yet reserved. She accepted it with a smile of quiet wonder. Mr. Quong nods before pedaling away, weaving through the bustling street.

Spider was passing by and tipped his hat. "Mr. Quong is a generous man."

Sena ran her fingers over the fine fabric of the bag, the weight of the unknown gift inside piquing her curiosity.

Jessie nudged her. "Don't just stand there—open it!"

Flustered, Sena looks down and opens the bag. Candy's inside. She reaches inside, chooses a piece, and plops it into her mouth. The smooth chocolate texture sends shivers of delight down her spine, a quiet "Mmmm" escaping her lips.

The ladies continue strolling downtown Missoula for another hour or two. Then headed back to The Gem Theatre for a performance only to find out they would not be performing this evening. Mr. Pierce had gone home. Frank Gates, Spider and Curly were standing at the bar.

"Curly?" Says Sena with a sheepish grin.

"Ohhh, do you fancy Curly?" Asks Daisy.

"No," Sena whispers.

Spider says, "Ladies, drinks?"

Pierce had given them all a free night. A carefree feeling lingered inside The Gem Theatre. Sounds of fireworks blasting throughout the late afternoon and into the night.

Swaying with his glass, Gates lifts his arm and says, "Let's all go out to the Fort!"

"Yes!" They all cheer in unison one after another.

Spider says, "I got to get my dog."

Gathering outside in the crisp mountain air, they felt the chill frosting at their cheeks. In the night's darkness, a strange lightness lingers—snow reflects a soft glow from the moon, feeling surreal at the early hour of 2 am. Gates shut and locked the back door, turning to Sena, Daisy and Jessie, who were generating warmth by rubbing their hands together. With a playful grin and a slight wobble from having indulged in a bit too much whiskey, Gates shouts in his thick Irish brogue, "Ah, c'mon, m'lovely lasses! Let's keep this Chinese New Year  shindig goin'! The night's still young, and so am I!" Melodically, the girls laughs. Peppering snow piling on their clothes as they gathered into a horse-drawn carriage. Gates takes the reins.

Settling into the sleigh, Curly stands with his back against the building smoking a cigarette, smoke rings puff upwards mixing with the peppering snow. Gates says, "Curly, hop in!"

Curly springs into the carriage beside the girls. Gates keeps pace with Spider, who sways unsteadily, struggling to walk alongside Tipple, his dog.

"C'mon, Spi—hop in. Help me lead the way..." Gates slows his words for emphasis. "Remember, we are going to the fort."
It's clear Spider is confused.

Fumbling, he locks eyes with Sena, flashing a flirtatiously forbidden smile. Then, with a grin, he and Tipple clamber into the carriage. "Lead the way," he says—then pauses, jabbing a thumb at his chest. "Wait! I'll lead the way." He straightens, his confidence returning, and proclaims it to the lively town, where fireworks crackle, lanterns' glow, and the sounds of Chinese New Year celebrations winding down echo through the streets.

Visibility decreases as the snow peppers. Their drunken state makes them feel invincible and in charge, yet prevents them from really driving the carriage. Meanwhile, Jessie lays down falling fast asleep. They take a wrong turn which leads them out to Bonner. Spider looks over and notices what he thinks is the Clark Fork River, "I think we missed the route to the Fort."

Curly pulls the reins. Frank jumps out. They rotate the carriage around that was getting stuck in the snow. Curly lets go of the reins for only a moment. The horses get skittish and take off without a driver. Jessie wakes up in the commotion standing and falls out of the carriage getting badly injured.

Spider's dog leaps out barking. Spider says, "Tipple! No!"

Spider tightly clutches the side of the carriage, reaching out to grab Sena to keep her from falling. Daisy and Curly cling on as the carriage lurches sideways, the sound of their screams filling the winter air. Sena and Spider tumble off the seats, landing in the cold, powdery snow. The scent of damp earth mingles with the metallic tang of blood as they realize they are all badly hurt. Frank rushes to his friends, the crunch of his boots in the snow the only sound as he quickly takes control. He mounts one of the horses, the leather creaking under his weight as he gallops back towards the city. The icy wind bites at his cheeks as he secures a hack and returns with aid, the relief palpable in the air.

Spider shouts out notably distressed, "Where is Tipple?"

The ride back into the city was long and painful. Spider carried Jessie up to her room—the worst of the injured—and laid her carefully on the bed before hurrying off to fetch some ice for her head.

Already intoxicated and in pain, Jessie reached for a bottle left behind by the room's former tenant. Without a second glance, she downs a mouthful, assuming the alcohol would dull her discomfort. Moments later, she doubles over, clutching her stomach, a strangled scream escaping her lips.

Doors creak open as the 3rd floor residents of the theater rush into the hallway.

"I think we need to fetch the doctor," Curly says.

Spider nods and bolts for help. Dr. Gwinn and Dr. Mills arrived quickly. Assessing Jessie's writhing form, they exchange grave glances.

"What did she drink?" Dr. Mills asks, the possibility of a suicide attempt flickering in his tone.

Jessie weakly pointed toward the bottle. Dr. Gwinn picks it up, studying the label.

Daisy, sobbing, shaking her head. "She would never!"

Dr. Gwinn turns to Dr. Mills, his expression grim. "Contaminated alcohol?"

Without hesitation, the doctors began pumping her stomach. Sena felt deeply shaken, with her heart pounding in her chest. The sight of Jessie fighting for her life brought back vivid memories of her mother's drunken episodes. The acrid smell of fear lingered in the air, making her body tense up involuntarily. Desperate for relief, she quietly tiptoes down the stairs, the creaking floorboards echo through the concert hall. Reaching the kitchen, she pours herself a glass of cool water, hoping to calm her nerves.

A faint scratching sound makes her pause. 'Tipple!' She whispered to herself. Opening the door, a rush of cool air carried the scent of damp earth and leaves. The sight of the dog, with his tail wagging eagerly and pressing against her legs, grounded her. They ventured back into the dimly lit bar, where the wooden floors creaked under their weight. Spider appeared weary at the top of the stairs.

"Tipple, my boy," Spider murmured, his rough voice softened as he affectionately tousled the dog's ears.

# Chapter 8

**February 1902, Missoula, Montana**

Silence grips The Gem Theatre as Frank Pierce begins tapping his gold cane and a rolled-up newspaper. The Gem Stock Company players, singers and staff shuffle into the grand hall. Pierce's commanding presence normally conveying warmth and cheer, yet today the atmosphere is crackling with tension. Nervous energy vibrates through the room, causing their hands to shake and quivering in their voices.

Pierce stands near the stage, arms crossed, repeating in his slow Texas drawl, "Go on, have a seat." The deep resonance of Pierce's voice echoed through the space, a sound like thunder rolling across a vast plain.

Settling into their seats, they could feel their hearts pounding, the air heavy with the unspoken fear and anticipation of what was to come.

One by one, they settled, the scrape of chairs against the wooden floor echoing in the hush. Some fidget, unable to keep still. Pierce's silence stretching the room taut. Sena arrives late, slipping into a chair at the back. The quiet was so profound that the faintest sounds—her skirt brushing her legs, the barely audible creak of wood—seemed to shatter the stillness.

Pierce let the silence sit a moment longer, then exhales sharply, his voice carrying an edge. "Do I treat y'all well?" He gazes around the room for a moment, his eyes sweep over them like a man taking stock of his herd. "Do I pay y'all fair?"

A few hesitant nods follow, some murmur affirmations.
Pierce's jaw tenses. "I closed the doors to my concert hall. I step away for one damned night to tend to personal matters, and what do I return to? A scandal—A scandal!"

Pierce gave a mirthless chuckle, shaking his head and throwing down the newspaper. "Have y'all read the headlines? Marshall Prescott's got himself a heyday sniffin' 'round, hopin' for somethin' to pin on me."

Pierce shot a sharp glance at Spider, a silent exchange passing between them.

Pierce continues, his voice low but firm. "This kinda foolishness makes folks think The Gem is a seedy dive, and that means empty seats, unsold tickets. And let me remind y'all of somethin' real clear—this ain't that kinda place. We're entertainers, not heathens, not drunkards, not ill-moral riffraff." He let the words sink in before adding, "Last thing we need is a raid!"

The silence was deafening. Repeat after me, "I am a moral, upstanding entertainer."

A chorus resounded, "I am a moral, upstanding entertainer."

Pierce nods, satisfied. "Now, let's show the city of Missoula who we really are—respectable folk who put on a damn fine show." He clapped twice, the sound cracking like a pistol shot. "Let's rehearse. Sena, you're up first."

Sena takes a deep breath, smoothing her skirt as she steps upon the stage. She begins to sing *The Swedish Nightingale*, her clear voice filling the space.

Pierce winced. "No, no, no." He shook his head, cutting her off. Sena flustered, confusion flickering across her face.

"That ain't gonna cut it." Pierce gestures vaguely toward the empty seats. "We need somethin' livelier. This is liable to put 'em straight to sleep." He turned abruptly. "Daisy?"

Daisy perked up. "Yes, Mr. Pierce?"

Pierce indicated Sena and Daisy before turning to Davenport with the request, "Give them a hand; devise a dazzling act. And teach Sena some stage directions."

Turning back to the stage, he exhales, rubbing his temple. "Gates, you're up next. After Gates—Gloie and Maud deliver your high-class duet, you promised." Clapping, "I demand excellence on this stage!"

As Gates made his way forward, Sena, Daisy, and Davenport slipped into the side room. Davenport hops upon a table, then swings his legs as he takes command of the room.

Davenport claps and says, "All right, ladies let's make this fun. Amusin'. Something that'll wake 'em up." He takes off his hat ] hands it to Sena. "Here. Use this as a prop. Let's get creative."

In the following week, after the worst had passed, Jessie was teasingly called 'Jaunty Jessie', although the jest did little to erase the memory of the ordeal.

Sena steps through the back door of The Gem, the chill of the morning air clinging to her skin, a washboard in one hand and a bucket in the other. She hears murmurs of hushed voices—Pierce, Davenport, and Spider—their voices reaches her as she approaches the back hall; a sense of secrecy hangs heavy in the air. She pauses, curiosity getting the better of her. She leans in closer to the wall. The walls are thin, making it easy to catch snippets of their conversation.

Davenport's sharp Boston accent cut through first. "—Yerrick's gotta make some kinda concession."

Spider's face conveys worry, "I owe him, lads. Were it not for 'im, I'd still be rottin' in a bloody jail cell. He has pull with Prescott."

Davenport huffed. "I get it, but we need—"

Pierce cut in, his Texan drawl firm. "Yer needed at The Gem. I'll pay Yerrick a visit, see if we can reach some kinda arrangement."

Spider let out a breath. "He'll be here tomorrow to settle the bill for our order. If I don't show up to work for him, he'll be in a right fury. He needs extra help at the bottling company since his attention is drawn to his new building going up and he's fit to be tied after the fire at his house last month."

Pierce rubs his head. "The Gem is your top priority. I need you making customers happy."

Spider pleads, "Can't ya ask Curly to stay another day?"

Pierce hesitates, rubbing his jaw. "Fine—but Curly's gotta get back to Great Falls soon."

Sena tiptoes backward, feigning nonchalance as the door creaks open and the men stepped out.

Pierce spots her first. "Well, hello there, Miss Sena! Davenport tells me that you and Daisy cooked up a fine number for us tonight."

Sena forces a bright smile and nods before slipping away up the stairs. But her thoughts lingered on what she had overheard. What kind of trouble had Spider been in? Jail? He did not seem the type. Then again, she had only scratched the surface of who he really was. She found herself thinking about his grin, the way he laughs—A sharp knock at the door jolts her from her thoughts. Embarrassed at where her mind had wandered, she hurried to answer.

Jessie steps in, Daisy right behind her.

"We have news!" the twins announced in unison.

Sena blinked. "What?"

"It's time for us to move on to the next place," Jessie says.

"Move on?" Sena repeated, stunned. "I thought you'd stay."

Jessie shrugs. "Oh, this was just temporary for us. A new show. A new city."

Daisy adds cheerfully, "Sena, you'll do great here. You've still got Gloie and Maud, for now, til they move on."

That night, the stage shimmering like a mirage with a golden glow of footlights. Sena and the rest of The Gem Stock Company moved like figures in a dream, their laughter and melodies weaving a spell over the theater. When Sena takes the stage with Daisy, she pours herself into the performance, every note, every step brimming with electric joy.

Then, as if conjured by some dazzling vaudeville fantasy, Daisy and Jessie took their last appearance on The Gem stage. They performed their popular act of a Cake Walk sending ripples of delight through the crowd.

As Sena stands upon the stage's wings, the applause reverberates for the twin duo: Daisy and Jessie.

Tears well up in Sena's eyes, shimmering with unshed emotions as she looked out at the sea of faces on the audience floor. The weight of impending loss of more people in her circle exiting hung heavy in the air. Sena feels deeply connected to people weaving invisible threads. When people exit too fast, too hurriedly, her heart chips. Her heart breaks because the twins will not be a constant in her life.

And Gloie and Maud? She hadn't spoken with them yet. Perhaps it was time to try.

After the show, Curly stands behind the bar, rinsing glasses, and setting them to dry. The warm glow of the concert hall lamps flickered across the polished wood, catching the swirl of smoke and laughter still lingering from the night's festivities.

Sena steps up to the bar, brushing a stray hair from her cheek. "Will you pour me a glass of water?"

"Sure thing, Miss Sena." Curly grabs a clean glass, fills it, and slides it toward her. "Sang real pretty this evening." Pausing for a moment, "I'm due back in Great Falls tomorrow. Best be restin' up."

Just then, the back door swung open, bringing a gust of cold night air with it. Spider strode in, his gait a touch unsteady, Tipple keeping pace beside him. Spider looked worn to the bone. Curly raised a brow. "Keep that up, and you're gonna keel over."

Spider waved him off with a tired grin. "Eh, I gotta keep me promises." He pulls out a chair, flopping into it. "You'll keel over 'fore I do, lad. But mark my words—we've gotta open a saloon together before we go in the ground."

Curly chuckles, wiping down the last glass. "Now that's a fine idea."

"Oh, boys, do not talk such foolishness." Sena rolls her eyes, and takes a sip of water.

Curly and Spider looked at her with a sense of seriousness.

"Oh, You two are serious?"

Spider's charisma fills the room, "Sena, my lass I may be daft, but I have enough gold in my heart to fill this stein." Spider then springs to his feet, throwing an arm dramatically in the air. "Aye! Curly & Spider's Saloon! The finest drinkin' establishment in all of Montana. We'll be the best bartenders this side of the divide!" He traces imaginary letters envisioning a future sign above a bar entrance.

Sena shakes her head with a small laugh.

Curly stretches his arms, stifling a yawn. "Well, it's been a grand time celebratin' the Chinese New Year, but I best lay down my head. Gotta catch the mornin' train."

Spider smirks. "Aye, your wife must be missin' ya somethin' fierce."

Curly shrugs. "Nah, she's in Idaho workin'."

They bid each other goodnight, Curly trots up the stairs, Spider lingering for a moment longer. Sena turns to go—but not before stealing one last look at him.

And Spider, for all his weariness—he pretends not to notice her longing glances at him. He pats Tipple's head and ears. "Good boy."

As Sena walks up the stairs of the theater to her room, she contemplates her inner thoughts about Curly and Spider. Curly is like a protective older brother, like the times he saved her when working at Christie's saloon. Spider is different. He makes her pulse quicken. His mysterious nature sparks her curiosity. She is confused.

Sena wonders, "Would I be frowned upon in society if I were to court a bartender?  Should I dare?"

# Chapter 9

**February 23, 1902, Missoula, Montana**

As the sun rose on the last Sunday morning of the month the aroma of eggs, sizzling bacon and freshly baked biscuits fill the room the theater. Cheerful chatter fills the room as Spider, Gloie, Maud and a few others gather around the table, their voices blend with the clinking cutlery. Amid it all, Mary Pierce moves gracefully, the faint sound of her footsteps mingling with the clatter of plates as she served breakfast, adding to the warm ambiance of the theater's community.

"Sena, come now, have a seat," Mary calls, waving her over. Sena slips into an empty chair as people passed plates of food to her. She bit into a biscuit—flaky, warm, and tasty.

Gloie grinning, held out a jar. "Strawberry jam?"

Sena's eyes light up. "Yes, please!" She finds Gloie's pronunciation of "jam" unusual; she uses a slight Southern accent.

Mary smiles beamingly, "an older woman here in Missoula makes it—city folk say it's the best preserves 'round." Pausing, she looks toward Sena. "Would you be willing to watch little Missoula this morning while Mr. Pierce and I attend the church service?"

Hesitation fell over Sena. She had little experience with babies. Before she could answer, Gloie clapped her hands together, "Of course she will! I'll help her."

Mary's face brightened. "You two are just wonderful. Thank you." She gently handed baby Missoula to Sena, who cradled her uncertainly.

Gloie cooed at the child. "I love how you named her after the city you live in—so charmin'."

Mary winking, "Frank and I fell in love in this magical city. You know, he wants Missoula to thrive," placing a hand on her hip and slightly leans onto the table, "Believes suitable entertainment makes for happy citizens. A powerful city is a prosperous city."

Gloie hands Missoula to Sena, who carefully carries the sleeping baby into the dimly lit rehearsal room toward the worn, wooden rocking chair in the corner. The old, slightly worn stage chair, typically just for show, proved unexpectedly useful that Sunday morning. The rhythmic swaying soothed the infant, whose tiny hand rested on the delicate eyelet trim of her white dress. Lavender trim at the dress's bottom brings Sena's memories of childhood lupine fields in Sweden to mind.

Gloie joined her shortly thereafter. She sat beside Sena in quiet companionship, the two women speaking in hushed tones between long stretches of silence, careful not to disturb the baby's slumber.

After a while, Gloie broke the stillness. "You're lucky, y'know. Bein' here at The Gem."

Sena whispers, "Why so?"

Gloie glances toward the door, then back at Sena. "Mr. Pierce is a different kind of manager. It's safe here," closing her eyes dramatically and opening them again.

"Safe?" Sena frowned.

Gloie's voice dropped lower. "Yea, many concert halls and theatre owners sell their girls to the highest bidder. Extra income in it, you know. You never know what kinda place you're walkin' into until you arrive, especially in the west"

Sena stiffens her posture. A memory washes over her—Christie's place, her mother forcing her to dance. The way Curly stood between and that seedy gentleman who tried grabbing her... Suddenly, she realizes why Mr. Holter had been so angry about her working there. Shame crept up her spine. She wonders if people look at her differently for being in a concert hall? Sena begins to question her morals. Sena swallows. "Oh my, I didn't realize."

Gloie smirks. "Figured as much. Maud says you was a bit naïve."

Sena, irritated, snaps, "I'm not nearly as *naïve* as you think. I was married to the great Owen Bockley, if you've heard of him."

Gloie's eyes widen. "The vaudeville comedian that went missin'? The one who—"

Sena gave a slow nod, rocking Missoula gently.

Gloie hesitates. "The one who left his wife high and dry? Oh, Miss Sena," Gloie sighs. "I am so sorry you fell for his wicked charms! Met him a couple of times on the circuit. He's slick and sly!"

Sena presses her hips together and exhales, her voice softer. "I am still quite new to the ways of America, to the world. I keep learning." She hummed, stroking Missoula's tiny hand. "Oh, Missy baby, you are a beautiful girl..."

Gloie smiles in a maternal sense, wiping a tear away, "She really, is..."

"What's—?" Sena asks, hearing footsteps in the background. "What's wrong?"

Gloie shrugs.

Frank and Mary Pierce walk into the room. Mary says, "Thank you, ladies, for watching Missoula."

Frank Pierce's jaw was tight, his steps clipped with agitation. He barely spoke as Sena handed baby Missoula to Mary.

Sena's brow creases with concern for Gloie and Frank Pierce. She feels something was amiss with both of them.

"Go on home, Mary." Pierce muttered.

Turning to Sena and Gloie, "We're holdin' a company meetin' at noon. Sharp. Gather everyone, immediately!"

Sena watches Mary's face as it tightens with worry, but she didn't press further. Sena passes Missoula to Mary and watches them exit.

As Sena goes about finding others, her stomach twists with concern and ponders Gloie's comments about being 'safe.'
For the next half hour, Sena frets relentlessly as the cast and crew gather in the concert hall, some lounging in the seats, others murmuring in hushed tones.

At last, Pierce and Davenport step upon the stage.

Pierce looks grim. He held a slip of paper in his hands, staring at it for a long moment before exhaling sharply. "You tell 'em," he says, handing the paper to Davenport.

The room fell silent.

Gloie leans over and whispers, "Did he lose The Gem? Is Sheriff Prescott shutting us down?"

Spider whispers, "Maybe Prescott, nah Pierce ain't gonna lose The Gem." Shrugging, he places his hand upon his knee. "It's gonna be another lecture."

Davenport unfolds the paper and reads aloud. "Dear Mr. Pierce, proprietor of The Gem Theatre, it is with great sadness that we must inform you that Galen Williamson, formerly under your employ, was found dead in his room in Great Falls."

Hushed gasps, cries and whispers roll through the air. A chair scrapes loudly against the floor.

With a pained expression, Spider shot up, grief etched on his face. In silence, he picks up a leftover prop cane, and flings it across the room. His eyes burn with rage as he stomps towards the door slamming it behind him. The sound echoes through the empty theater. Outside, the wind's fury mirrors the storm within him.

Sena jolts at the outburst. She turns to Gloie, whispering, "Who... who is Galen Williamson?"

Gloie shrugged her shoulders, devoid of emotion.

Around them, many wept, faces etched with sorrow. Yet many with no to little emotion. A deep pit forms in her stomach.

Davenport's voice was thick with emotion. "We'll be closin' the theater tonight so everyone can grieve in their own way." He swallowed hard. "Curly was one of us. Even after he left, he came back often. He helped whenever he could. We must take our time to grieve—then the show must go on."
Sena's breath hitches.

*Curly?*

*Dead?*

*No. He was young. Strong. Able-bodied. Dead?*

Shock runs through Sena's body. She wonders what happened. Before she knew it, she runs up the stairs, down the hall, and into her room. The door slams shut behind her, and she throws herself upon the bed.

**Her inner monologue takes over as she processes the news of Curly's death:**
Curly was a good man. A kind man. Curly saved me all those years ago. A steady hand in an unsteady world. Liquor hadn't taken him, not even on the wildest nights. Even during the Chinese New Year, he'd been the soberest among them. He and Spider were going to open a saloon together. The news must devastate Spider. Oh, poor Spider.

Sena curls into herself, silent sobs wracking her body. Drifting off to sleep for several hours. She wakes up to the sound of muffling sobs. The walls were thin, grief seeping through them like smoke. Her stomach aches with hunger, so she lights a candle and slipped quietly down the hall to the theater's kitchen. There, she finds Frank Gates hunched over the counter, chewing on a leftover biscuit from breakfast.

As he looks up, he speaks through the bite, his Irish lilt thick with weariness. "These biscuits, Sena—they're a fine remedy for a broken heart. Nothin' like flour and butter to feed the emotional toil of a man." He swallows and tilts his head. "Can't sleep a wink, eh?"

Sena shakes her head, and sinks into a chair as Gates slides a biscuit her way.
"I wish I had some wit about me," he sighs. "But even comedians sink deep into sadness. I didn't know the lad that well."

They sat in heavy silence, the air thick with loss. The candle flickers between them, barely holding back the shadows. After a moment, Gates glances at her. "You didn't know it was Curly at first, did you?"

Sena's throat tightens. She shakes her head.

"Yeah… not just you, lass. Everyone knew him as Curly. Reckon you weren't the only one in that room who didn't know his true name." Gates sighs as he runs a hand through his unkempt hair.

A sudden clatter rings from outside. Bang. Clang. Bang. Clang. Then, the back door flew open. Spider stumbles through the door frame, reeking of whiskey, his boots dragging against the floor. Tipple barks from across the theater, his paws clicking against the oak floors as he rushed to Spider's side. The dog whines, nuzzling against him, sensing Spider's distress.

Gates was on his feet in an instant, grabbing Spider by the shoulders, steadying him. "Easy now, lad. You'll be knockin' down the whole damn kitchen."

Spider sways, his breath ragged. "Damn fool's dead… how can he be dead? We gotta open a saloon."

"Come on," Gates murmurs, his grip firm. "Let's get you up to bed before you fall flat on your arse."

Sena watches as Gates half-carried Spider out of the kitchen, Tipple whining and trotting at their heels. The last thing she saw was Spider's grief-stricken face before they disappeared into the darkened halls.

She finishes her biscuit, brushes the crumbs from her hands, and picks up her candle. As she makes her way back to her room, she notices a figure sitting alone in the theater. Frank Pierce. He sits in the dim glow of the oil lamps, his broad shoulders slumped, a glass in hand. His somber face shows the weight of sorrow clings to him.

Sena thinks, "Aww, Pierce cares about all of us." In that moment, she realizes Curly's death was actively wrecking him. She hesitates before going up the stairs.

Pierce lifts his gaze, he catches her stare.

"Starin' at a sad man, eh?" His voice was rough, but there is no anger in it. "Come, sit."

"Oh, no, I—" Sena says tongue-tied.

Pierce gives a tired shrug.

"Come on," patting the chair, "Come sit."

As Sena takes her seat, Pierce continues. "Can't figure you out, Sena. Bold and courageous one minute, shy the next." He studies her for a moment, then asks, "You knew Curly from your time in Butte?" Accentuating the "u" in Butte with his Texas draw.

She almost smiled because of his southern draw, which she found charming and new to her experience in America. She nods, swallowing against the lump in her throat. "Yes... My mother had me working for Christie Leutner."

Pierce's eyes narrow, listening and nods as he takes another drink.

Sena continues. "Curly protected me from an ill-moraled man." Her voice cracks as she wipes a tear from her cheek.

Pierce exhales, shaking his head. "I have rules against that type of behavior. It's why I have a guard in my employ stationed at the entrance." Momentary silence as he swirls the liquid in his glass. "Curly was a good man, indeed. A damn shame. So young. Too damn young." He set his glass down and stood. "I best be gettin' home to Mary and little Missoula."

Sena nods, watching as he turns to leave.

But then, he pauses at the door. "Hey, Sena." His voice was firm. "If any man tries somethin' on you here—you run to Spider, you hear? He'll look after you. Same as Curly did." He gestures to the empty theater. "This is a happy place. I want people to feel joy. Nothin' but joy." And with that, he disappears into the night.

Sena stood there, turning over his words.

**_Joy._**

As Sena climbs the stairs to her room she thinks about Gloie's comments about theater proprietors. As she lands at the second floor balcony she gazes at the private booths. She realizes Pierce cares about more than about the people in his employ than a full house and ticket sales. As she makes each step to the third floor, she feels Pierce spoke about joy as if it were something sacred. She wishes for joy. She wishes a magician could pull a ribbon from his sleeve and deliver joy to her.

*West Front Street, Missoula, Montana. The Gem Theatre sign, far left.*

# Chapter 10



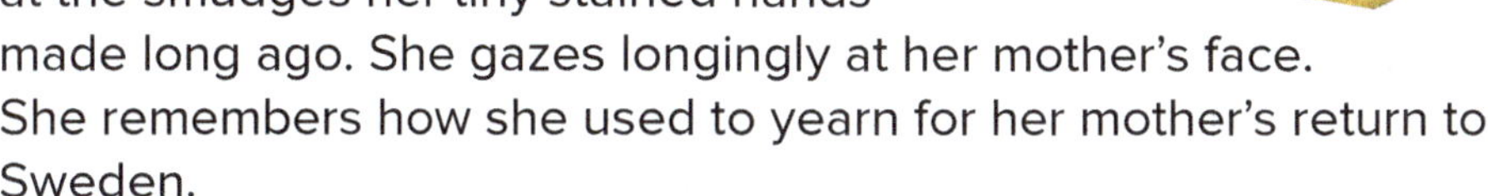

$S$itting on a chair inside her room, she reaches inside a drawstring purse. Sena grasps a stained tintype of her mother. Tracing its worn edges with her fingers. Fixating on the purple and black stains she made as a child. Visions of her younger self flood her mind; she recalls running through the grass as a child, squeezing lupine flowers firmly. She recalls lying in the vast fields, feeling drained of energy. She hears sounds of rustling leaves and chirping birds. She stares at the smudges her tiny stained hands made long ago. She gazes longingly at her mother's face. She remembers how she used to yearn for her mother's return to Sweden.

The ache from missing her mother stirs her to write to her mother. None of her previous letters had been returned. Still, she wrote, hoping for a reply. The ache in her chest intensifies as she picks up a pen, each stroke on the paper a physical manifestation of her mother's absence. Tears well up in her eyes, blurring the words on the page as she pours her heart in the letter. The weight of her emotions are a heavy burden. Her shoulders begin to slump and her body trembles with each word she pens. Despite the uncertainty of receiving a reply, the act of writing is a cathartic release, a way to bridge the gap between them even if only through paper and ink. The ache is a constant reminder of her yearning. This ache drives her to keep reaching out. She writes to the Holter's, too. Thinking—surely, they would do her the courtesy of returning her post. She addresses it to them, carefully copying the address, "Berkeley, California."

A day off from performing—it was a rare chance to run errands. First, stopping at the post office, noting the cost of postage in her diary—four cents total, two cents per stamp. The small price of reaching out, of trying to mend frayed connections. Afterward, she takes a stroll through Missoula's streets. Evident of growth, the city is bustling with construction projects dotting every corner—foundations being laid, inspections conducted, surveyors measuring plots, builders hammering and hauling materials. It seemed that everywhere she turned, someone is preparing for something new.

A woman with a flower in a small pot smiles and waves to her as she turns the corner onto Cedar and Stevens Streets. Sena then noticed the foundation of a new building as she passed by. What would it become? Her imagination wondered—A store? A boarding house? The Newbro Drug Company sign on Main Street caught her attention, and she was greeted by the clerk's bright smile as she entered the store. "Greetings, miss. What shall I assist you with today?"

"Ja, I'd like some of the imported perfume?" She asks.

"Why yes, step this way. Here is our selection of the finest imported perfumes," the clerk says, motioning toward a glass display case. Leaning in, Sena opens several bottles, inhaling their subtle fragrances. While she pondered her options, the door opened with a jingle.

"Why, hello, Sena! You must try this cheese.  Oh, and the fruit I just purchased—it's super da—lish!" With a rush and a flurry of northern and southern-tinged words, Gloie excitedly chattering as she entered the shop.

"Oh? Where did you find it?" Sena replies.

"Kelley and Edwards, I believe." Pointing, "It's over yonder in the Feddersohn Block. Some of the best groceries I've seen in my travels on the circuit," Gloie says, picking up a bottle of perfume and sniffing it.

"Mmmm," Sena sniffed the ornate blue decorated bottle, handing it Gloie to take a whiff as well.

"Ahhh, what a divine scent!" Gloie says, eyes wide, showing the bottle.

Sena chuckles, shaking her head as they both burst into laughter as they both select perfume.

Sena looks at a brooch. Gloie is looking at some toys. Gloie seems lost in thought, her eyes almost teary. The emotional turmoil that Gloie is experiencing is clear in her physical appearance. The usual sparkle in her eyes is gone, replaced by unshed tears that hint at sadness or deep thought. Her forehead lines crease. The weight of her feelings seems to hang heavy in the air around the toy jacks she is holding. Whatever thought saddens Gloie, it is affecting her posture and demeanor.

Sena thinks about asking Gloie, yet decides against it.

They both gather a few other sundries, stopping to pay the clerk, exiting the store together.

Sena turns to Gloie. "My next stop is the Missoula Free Library. Would you care to join me?"

Gloie smiles. "Might as well, since I am staying in Missoula a little longer. Might be prudent to entertain my eyes."

Sena frowns. "So, you're not staying at The Gem?"

Gloie grins. "Oh, heavens no! This is a temporary stay." Laughing coily, "Never stay anywhere too long. Hopin' to join a company that travels the vaudeville circuit again. The Gem Stock Company is nice, safe, steady. I love adventure. Promised Maud I'd sing duets here and at other Montana joints, then back to the east coast I go!"

"East coast?" Disappointment washes over Sena's face.

Gloie smiling. "Ah, yes, I love the New York shoreline, don't you? It's divine—"

Sena interrupts. "Oh! I've never been. How do you pronounce your name? Saw it listed on the program. Wasn't quite sure."

Gloie laughing and playfully tossing her head back, "This question is as old as time." Moving a stray hair out of her eyes, "My momma always explained it like this—a candle's glow and how candy's gooey." Clasping her hands, "Put it together like pattycake and it's Glow-eey."

As they climb the stairs of the library entrance, the ladies laugh as Sena pronounces Gloie—GLOW—EEY. The library is a quiet environment, hushing their laughter. The scent of old paper and polished wood fills the air. They peruse the shelves. A copy of *The Missoulian* newspaper on the table. Gloie picks it up and smiles widely.

"Whatever has you joyful?" Sena asks.

"Roller Skating club in New York." Gloie beaming, lifting her arms and legs swaying in the motion of skating. "I was a champion skater in my teenage days!"

Sena looks at Gloie with surprise.

Approaching the front desk, the librarian peers at them over her small glasses and places a paper on the counter. "Ladies, here is an application. A community member must vouch for you prior to borrowing a book."

Sena sighs brushing her hand across her brow. "Oh, Ja, I had hoped to obtain a book today."

"The rules are the rules," states the librarian unmoved.

Turning towards the doors, Mary Pierce appeared from the stacks, bouncing baby Missoula on her hip. "Why, Miss Sena and Miss Gloie, what a pleasant surprise! Why are you leaving without a book in hand?"

 "The rules. We need someone to vouch for us," Gloie sneers.

Mrs. Pierce scoffs, placing her hand upon her heart. "Oh, heavens! I'll vouch for you both. I trusted you with my little one, did I not?" With that, they marched back to the counter.

The librarian's lips pressed into a thin line as she reluctantly checked out their books.

As they exit, Mary Pierce adjusts baby Missoula on her hip and speaks louder for the librarian to hear, "You need to see our vaudeville shows to understand the high caliber of our acts." They all step outside.

Gloie looking up, "I think I'll miss this beautiful western sky."

Mary Pierce walks towards her carriage. "I'm headed to The Gem to meet Frank. He's meeting with an architect for our new home. Where else are you ladies planning to go?"

Sena and Gloie exchange glances. "Back to The Gem."

"Well then, by all means, join me in the carriage. Save your energy for your performances."

As the carriage comes to a full stop, Spider is walks down the sidewalk. He promptly helped them out of the carriage by extending a hand.

In response, Mary says, "Thank you, Spider."

"Certainly, Mrs. Pierce," Spider nods and reaching for the other ladies' hands.

"Where have you been off to on your rare day off?" Mary asks.

"I was at an Eagles meeting," Spider replies.

"Oh, that's correct—you belong to the Eagles. Very noble of you." Mary compliments Spider.

Sena makes a mental note of this. This reminder her of Owen, her former husband. Owen was a member of the Eagles. Her mind drifts to the man she made eyes with at the Eagles benefit in Deadwood. She thinks, "What do these men have in common that I find appealing?" Perhaps it was a coincidence, but she found it strange.

Frank Pierce was inside, standing over large rolls of paper containing architectural drawings. He was discussing matters with another man. He looks up, makes a motion for Mary to join him.

"Oh, Mary, come, come. Over here. Meet Mr. Gibson—he's the

grand designer of our new home."

Mr. Gibson nods politely. "Hello, Mary, lovely to meet you. I'm your architect. Mr. Pierce has shared the instructions you provided for the home. Let's go over the plans."

While the Pierces discuss the blueprints, Sena and Gloie settle in at another table, nibbling cheese and reading.

Employees—actors and actresses going to and fro, lounging in the hall, having sidebar conversations throughout the late afternoon and evening. Sena notices Gloie get upset and gather her things after one of the acrobatic men took a knife out of his pocket to cut an apple. The distress on Gloie's face alarms Sena.

As the evening wore on, Mrs. Pierce and Missoula left for home, and Mr. Gibson took his leave.

Sena, however, found herself distracted. She watches Pierce wander towards the bar, leaning in close to Spider. She was not in earshot to hear everything, but she caught fragments—new arrivals at the hotel, extra security for this week's lineup. Were they talking about Spider's predicament with a man named Yerrick again? Something was going on, and whatever it was, it had the air of importance.

The Gem Theatre pulses with life every evening, whiffs of whiskey and cigar smoke curling through the air beneath the low gaslights. Sena weaves through the bustling crowd, skirts brushing against table edges, the clatter of glassware mingling with bursts of laughter. A typical show night—the kind where faces blur and voices blend.

Between acts, she has the chance to work the floor, clearing tables and collecting extra tips. But she hesitates, lingering between the back hall and the bar. One man stands out.

Her gaze locks on his face and demeanor—a man with a sharp, assessing stare. He sits alone at a corner table, relaxed yet commanding, like someone who belongs wherever he pleased. But the way others glanced at him—respectful, wary—tells her he is no ordinary patron.

"William A. Carlton," Spider murmurs as he stacks a tray with fresh drinks. "High-stakes gambler. Pockets deep as the mines—when he's winning." He smirks adjusting his grip.

Sena clung to her spot, fingers tracing the sequins on her costume as she watched Carlton lean toward Spider, speaking in low tones. Patrons at The Gem often pour their sorrows into Spider's ear as freely as he poured whiskey into their glasses. Spider listened to men's troubles as he filled their steins. But Carlton was different. He lingered, spoke little, listened much.

As the night wore on, performers wove through the crowd, clearing tables and hoping for loose change. Spider, ever the showman, worked the floor with his usual flair. Sena admires his skill—balancing twenty-seven full glasses on a single tray without a spill, a feat that seemed to defy reason. She watches as a patron plucks the first glass from the tray, allowing Spider to effortlessly slide the rest into place.  Later, she sees him gather an impossible number of empty steins—forty, maybe fifty—stacking them with the ease of a magician.

The flickering sconces catch the luster of his thick black hair, and Sena stares. There is a beauty to him amongst his ruggedness, not merely in his features but in the effortless grace with which he moved—an artist with glassware, a master of the room's pulse. He balanced stemmed goblets between his fingers, lined them along his forearms, and never faltered. And all the while, he smiled, laughed, charmed. Though he never sets foot upon the stage, he is, without question, apart of every evening's grand performance at The Gem. Spider is an act all his own.

Everyone looks towards disturbance near the staircase. Descending from the upper floor, a man stomped loudly while complaining. "Ain't right, charging more up there! Fees escalate the higher up you go."

Carlton, still nursing his own drink, scoffs, a slow chuckle escapes his lips. "Man's hunting for cheap spirits in the wrong place," he mutters, shaking his head.

Spider barely blinks, setting a glass down in front of Dave Kelsey— the electrical magic man, a performer whose tricks left audiences gasping. With a nod to Kelsey, Spider turned back to the griping customer, hands on his hips, his grin never wavering.

"Well now," Spider says, smooth as a winning hand. "If it's cheap you're after, there's a fine watering hole down the street. But if you're drinking here, might as well do it right."

The customer grumbles and sits down at Carlton's table.

Sena looks at Carlton. She notices him watching Spider, his expression mysterious. Then Carlton meets Sena's gaze. Sena senses Carlton is interested in more than just whiskey and cards, which made her uneasy.

## April 1902, Missoula, Montana

Sena's nerves tangled inside her stomach as she prepared for her evening performance. This was unlike anything she had done before—more alluring, more suggestive, though never revealing. Mr. Pierce's inspiration for a skit came from watching her and Gloie read. Onstage, Sena, in a flowing nightgown, was to appear lost in a book while lounging on a chaise lounge. Then, rising and twirling, she would sing and stir, holding *Hawthorne's Blithedale Romance*. The performance began. A hushed crowd heightened her pulse, The swelling music consumed her. The melody of her voice magically filling the hall. The audience erupts in cheers. One man in particular used some vulgar words. She carries on singing, nervously.

### *Reaching for Reveries*
A lively, yet wistful vaudeville tune with an uplifting melody.
**Verse 1**
*I like to read, to fill my mind,*
*With stories grand of every kind.*
*A world beyond this toil and strain,*
*Where dreams take flight and dull the pain.*
**Chorus**
*Reverie, reverie, lift me up so high,*
*Turn my sorrows into stars, let my spirit fly!*
*Reaching for reveries, breaking free at last,*
*Casting away the hurt— the troubles of my past.*
**Verse 2**
*Oh, wide wide world, so much to see,*
*Novels and dreams, I, I, I can be carefree!*
*A hero bold,*
*A dancer bright,*
*A soul unchained in golden light.*
**Repeat Chorus**
**Outro – Softly, then swelling to a grand finish**
*A warm embrace, no, let me go,*
*Beyond my pain, oh, let it snow.*
*Reverie, reverie, shining like the sunny sea,*
*A book's embrace, a mindful space, where I can truly be!*

As the curtains close, a whispered, octave-descending "Reverie" repeated softly a man from the audience grabs Sena's wrist and pulls her towards him. Frank Gates, Comedian, who stands in the wings intervenes, pulling her back from the man's hold. Dave Kelsey, electrician stands near the orchestra acts quickly by pulling the man back. A guard in The Gem's employ ejects from the theater.

Gloie and Maud run up to Sena backstage. Gloie asking, "Are you okay, darling? Some spectators are vulgar pigs!"

The next day, late into the night, the dim glow of lanterns flickered over a table where William Carlton and several other men were deep in a game of chance. Laughter and the clinking of glasses filled the air as actors and actresses unwound in the hallway after a long night of rehearsal.

Carlton smirks as he wins, while O'Hanlon, an out-of-towner, with a short temper and growing losses, becomes restless. Round after round, Carlton's luck holds steady, while O'Hanlon's dwindles. Spider keeps the drinks flowing, fueling both mirth and misery.

O'Hanlon scowls, his face flushed from drink and frustration. Finally, he shoves back his chair, staggering to his feet. "I'm out," he spits, his voice thick with resentment.

As O'Hanlon turns, his bloodshot eyes caught sight of a shadow—a woman slipping down the hallway toward the back of The Gem. He narrows his gaze, convinced she was a showgirl, the kind he assumes could be bought for the right price. A smirk curls his lips. Glancing around to make sure no one is watching; he follows the woman's path.

The dressing room door creaks as he steps inside. Maud stands in the lamplight, half-dressed, her back to O'Hanlon as she folds a costume. Gloie turns at a creaking sound, her expression shifting from exhaustion to alarm.

Meanwhile, out front, Carlton cheerfully gathers his winnings, clapping Spider on the back as he prepares to leave. "Goodnight, gentlemen," he announces, practically glowing with triumph.

Spider smirks and shakes his head as we wipes the steins dry with a towel, "Carlton had a lucky night. Bet you a dollar he loses it all by the end of the week."

Pierce chuckles, but before he can respond, a shriek rings out from the back. The laughter and straightforward conversation in the saloon falters, giving way to the unmistakable sound of a struggle - furniture scraping and alarmed voices.

Suddenly, O'Hanlon bursts from the hallway, his face twists in outrage. Accusingly, he bellows, finger shaking towards the dressing rooms, "Those women took $230 from me!"

Spider straightens his back, his usual relaxed demeanor sharpening into something cold and dangerous. "Excuse me?"

O'Hanlon jabbed a finger into his own chest. "They stole my money! I paid, and all I got was a goddamn shove off! I expect my money's worth of female companionship."

A tense silence settles over the room. Spider exchanges a glance with Pierce. Their non-verbal cues communicate something is awry. "Take it up with our proprietor, Mr. Pierce," Spider says coolly nodding towards Pierce. Then nodding at Dave Kelsey who runs to get Davenport.

Pierce steps forward, exuding an air of quiet authority. "May I help you?"

The burly security guard at the front door comes and stands behind Frank Pierce in support.

O'Hanlon's mouth twists. "Your girls stiffed me," he says, voice slurring with anger. "I want my damn roll of dollars back."

Pierce, ever the diplomat, forces a patient smile. "I think there has been a mistake. My girls do not engage in that kind of business."

O'Hanlon's face darkens. "Then I'll be back—with the law."

Sena hears the commotion from her room. Cautiously, she goes down the stairs and finds Frank Pierce, Maud, Gloie, and Frank Carroll. Furiously Carroll holds Gloie snugly, rocking her gently. The way he is holding her seems oddly intimate, causing Sena to take a second glance.

Pierce drops into a chair, rubbing his temples. "What happened?" Maud was the first to speak, her voice shaking. "I was putting away my costume stark naked behind the dressing curtain, and the next thing I knew, that filthy drunk was grabbing at my leg—"

Gloie cut her off, voice taut, "I yanked him back by his coat. Got him away from her."

Their words tumble over one another, both Gloie and Maud speak rapidly making it hard to understand. Gloie's speech accelerates faster and faster until it is unintelligible due to hysterics. Sena makes out Gloie's description of how afraid she was about the man pulling a knife on her.

Pierce exhales slowly and calmly, "Stop. One at a time." Motioning his hands from high to low. "He's claiming you took money for services—some of which weren't rendered."

Maud let out a bitter mocking laugh, covering her mouth as if the accusation itself was enough to make her sick.

Gloie's expression hardens. "That bastard!"

Carroll's face darkens to near purple. "I'll kill that son of a—"

Gloie places her hand upon Carroll's shoulder, "Now, Frank, really I will be okay."

Pierce raises his hand and extends his arm outward, "Let's stay calm, calm, calm."

Sena hesitates, then steps closer to Gloie. "I'm so sorry this happened to you."

Maud scoffs, "Little Miss Naïve chimes in, huh?"

Gloie shoots Maud a hard look. "Enough." Then, softening, she turns back to Sena, whispering "My love here is so furious he might hurt 'em."

Sena blinks. "Your *Love*?"

Gloie chuckles nonchalantly. "Yes. Frank Carroll and I are married."

She winks. "I use a stage name."

Sena's eyes widen and lips parted in surprise, "Ohh."

Once the chaos subsided and the details were ironed out, everyone went home or up to their quarters except Spider and Mr. Pierce, who were decompressing.

Spider leaning on the bar hand on his head, "What are you fixin' to do?"

Frank Pierce shakes his head. "I must clear their names. For them. For us. For the whole damn vaudeville circuit!"

Before Spider could utter a response, the front doors swung open with momentum. Sheriff Prescott strode in, O'Hanlon trailing behind him with a smug expression.

Prescott's voice carries across the room. "I've been told there's been a robbery here tonight, Pierce."

Pierce stands slowly. "Sir, you're mistaken. No robbery here."

Prescott's eyes gleaming with satisfaction. "I'm here to arrest the women who robbed Mr. O'Hanlon."

Pierce's jaw clenched. "On what evidence?"

A smirk plays on Prescott's lips. A chance to imprison Pierce or someone from The Gem has finally arrived, after a long wait. O'Hanlon's accusation provides him with justification.

Sena, gripped by icy fear, rushes to look over the railing and down the stairs, she clutches the banister as she hears the commotion. Sena thinks, *"Arrested? This is unbelievable."*

Sheriff Prescott pulls Gloie and Maud towards the door. Their screams sliced through the concert hall like a knife.

Pierce's fury simmers, his restraint unraveling.

As the sheriff hauls the women outside, Pierce turns abruptly, grabs a sack of flour from behind the bar, and drives his fist into it. A white cloud explodes into the air, dusting the room in a fine, ghostly powder. Then Pierce sits on the floor calmly, head bowed.

Spider goes over to Pierce and extends a hand to help Pierce back up. "Mark my words, Pierce. Dinna worry. We are gonna get 'em out and clear their name."

For Pierce it was the only thing he could hit that would not hit back.

*The Gem Theatre, West Front Street, Missoula, Montana.*

# Chapter 11

**April 1902, Missoula, Montana**

Pierce confidently walks into Mr. Yerrick's office, tipping his hat as he steps inside. Pierce declares, in his steady Texan accent, his intention to pay Spider's debt.

Yerrick glances up from his desk a few times. He shuffles a few papers before he leans back in his chair. He exhales through his nose as he sets his pen down. "Ain't that simple. The arrangement includes Spider workin' for me. That's how we set the interest, Pierce."

"I need him full time at The Gem. Spider draws crowds just as much as my performers," Pierce says, resting his hands on his belt.

Yerrick raises an eyebrow. "Sorry, no can do. I need him here. He has a debt and he's useful."

"How much to clear it outright?" Pierce asks, his voice steady.

Yerrick shakes his head. "You could pay it off today, but mark my words, you'll be coverin' for him again before long. Man's got a habit of landin' himself in trouble."

Pierce's lips pressed into a thin line. "He has been staying out of trouble. He's sobering up and steering clear of the mess rabble-rousers."

Yerrick lets out a low chuckle. "Maybe. Or maybe it's just a matter of time." He studies Pierce for a moment before adding, "You probably think I'm cold-hearted."

Pierce met his gaze. "Not at all. This is business."

Yerrick nods approvingly. "Speakin' of business, you hear about the new group of businessmen? Putting together the Business Men's Protective Association of Missoula. Helps deal with folks slow to pay their debts. You oughta come to a meetin'."

Pierce tilts his head. "Duly noted. Say, Mary mentioned your daughter's still unwell."

Yerrick's expression softens. "Aye. Zetta's heart ain't what it should be. Doctors say it doesn't pump proper."

Pierce nods solemnly. "Sorry to hear about this misfortune. I hope your daughter gets some relief."

Yerrick, clearing his throat, shifts the conversation. "You usin' Gibson as your architect for the house? How's that comin' along?"

Pierce's eyes show a hint of brightness. "Gonna be a grand home. Puttin' in a playground, too. Not just for my own kids, but for the neighborhood young'uns to enjoy."

Yerrick lets out a short laugh. "Always tryin' to bring joy to everyone, eh, Pierce? Even the littles." He leaned forward. "Reason I ask about Gibson—he's workin' on my bottlin' and liquor company building. Debatin' the number of stories. I'd like to go as high as possible, but it's takin' too damn long. I'll be lookin' for construction bids soon."

Pierce fiddles with his hat. "You'll have a grand buildin', no doubt."

Yerrick smirks. "Won't be as magical as The Gem, though. Walkin' in there's like steppin' into a dream. Hard to believe you pack in 800 folks."

Pierce winks. "People want magic?" Extending his arms. "Magic is what I do well! Told you when I came here it was gonna be a grand dream land. Made my dream come true—entertainin' the masses."

Yerrick's eyes widen with delight. "And indeed, you do! I suppose I'll allow you to pay off Spider's debt. He's a good lad—he gets into the damnedest trouble. Sometimes it's not even his fault. Wrong place, wrong time."

Pierce obliges, "Thank ya—I'll keep my eye on him."

Yerrick, "You're lucky to have him. So, what's this I hear about girls turning tricks at your fine establishment?"

Pierce's posture stiffens, waves his arms, sighs, and releases his breath. Shaking his head, "Mark my words, witnesses will prove their innocence!"

Yerrick lets out a deep belly laugh. "This one's really got you all worked up, hasn't it?"

Pierce shakes his head. "This man is making false claims, calling my employees liars. He is a deadbeat from out-of-town making false accusations. You know damned well I have a reputable concert hall."

Yerrick, "Best of luck to you, Pierce."

Pierce grabs his gold cane and nods. He stands up and turns to exit. As he reaches the door, he turns back to Yerrick. "We will make a gentleman out of Spider, eh?"

Behind bars, Gloie and Maud seethe with fury. The accusations are a blatant lie, and they despise being dragged into such a humiliating ordeal. When their court date arrived, many witnesses stepped forward, testifying in their favor. The defense claimed the man had fabricated this claim. It was his word against theirs.

The courts rule Gloie and Maud are innocent, yet the sting of false accusation lingers. This experience leaves them feeling humiliated. They feel shame due to the newspaper reports. They decide to leave The Gem earlier than planned. Sena accompanies Gloie and Frank Carroll to the depot to see them off.

Gloie squares up, places her hands upon Sena's shoulders and locks eyes. "Wise up girl. This world may appear dreamlike, you have to watch out for the dampenin' evil."

Tears streaming down Sena's cheeks, "You have taught me much about life in these few short weeks."

"And you should know that sly Owen. He didn't deserve someone like you," Gloie reassures. "If he resurfaces, keep him at bay. Wipe your hands of that mess."

Sena nods, crying.

Gloie tilted her head and waved her hand, "Now, now, stop sprinklin' water from those dream filled eyes. It's not all evil out there. Stay naïve, promise me—stay naïve."

They laugh in unison.

Sena says, "I'll miss you."

Gloie imparts vaudeville circuit business wisdom, "In this business, we don't miss one another. We come. We go. We perform. We move on." Patting her heart, "Keep me in here until I show up on stage with you again."

Sena notices a toy sticking out of Gloie's satchel. She asks, "Who is the toy for?"

Gloie tears up and hugs Sena once more. The train whistle blows. Gloie whispers, "My sons."

Sena quietly gasps and eyes widen, "sons?"

Gloie nods and runs toward the train leaving Sena on the platform.

Sena nods and waves as Frank Carroll and Gloie load the train. She watches as the train leave the station; her heart feels heavy.

Inside The Gem, the lamps cast a warm glow. Sena sits at a table, her keen eyes scan the room, ears attune to all conversations. She has a knack for observing, picking up on even the subtlest exchanges.

New actresses shuffle in to take Gloie and Maud's place. As Sena sizes them up, she dismisses the notion of friendship. The new recruits are all show and no substance—flashy, fake, and empty-headed. A fresh lineup for Pierce and Davenport to manage, and the two men are already hard at work at the empty bar, sorting out the details.

Spider trods in, his expression a mix of curiosity and disbelief. "Pierce, did you really paid off my debt to Yerrick?" He asks, gripping the back of a chair.

Pierce nods nonchalantly. "Indeed, I did. Don't let me down. Stay outta brawls and mayhem." His tone is firm and laced with trust. Spider picks up a glass, rolling it between his fingers before nodding in agreement.

Davenport leans forward. "Did Yerrick share any news about his building? Will they ever finish building it?

Pierce grins. "Yeah, he's looking for construction bids."

Davenport smirks. "Good. Can't just be a foundation forever at the corner of Stevens and Higgins. It's liable to turn into a stone promenade instead of a bottling and liquor company."

Sena notices the gambler William Carlton has become a fixture at The Gem after a recent high stakes win. He is always at the bar, bragging to Spider about his lucky streak. There were likely other regulars she fails to notice. Many nights, The Gem is packed with a couple of hundred patrons. Yet, she feels increasingly out of step with the new crowd. Her conversations with comedian, Frank Gates, are growing less frequent.

A man arrives with the day's post. Sena takes it upon herself to distribute the mail.

Davenport smirks as she approaches. "You're getting to be a regular at this, Sena. Anything for me?"

She flips through the stack. "Why, yes, a letter addressed to you."

Taking the envelope, Davenport's expression brightens. "Ah, from a military pal of mine. Back in my Civil War days. He's been acting in New York. I'm hoping to persuade him to travel west and perform here. The West can be a frightful thing to Easterners."

Sena nods absently, continuing through the stack. "Something for Spider. Have you seen him?"

"Yeah, he's in the back, sorting the liquor delivery."

She makes her way towards the storeroom. Rounding the corner, she blurts out, "Spider—" then stops abruptly, her breath catching. There he was, locked in a kiss with one of the new actresses.

Spider pulls away, eyes wide with guilt. "Uh, Sena. What can I do for you?"

Awkwardly, she extends the letter. "You have a post."

"Thank you, Miss Sena," as he stretches his arm wide to take it from her.

She pivots quickly on her heel, rolling her eyes, feeling vaguely disgusted. Continuing to sort the remaining mail, she comes across a letter from the Holter's and slips it into the pocket of her dress. Later, as she passes through The Gem, she hears some of new girls cackling, followed by the unmistakable sounds of pleasure from the upstairs rooms.

Sena steps outside to wash her clothes. Her mind is on Spider.

Mrs. Pierce steps out the back door of The Gem, a fresh bouquet of flowers in her hands. "Sena, there you are. I need some assistance with the costumes." Mary takes note of Sena's somber expression, Mary asks, "What has you so glum, dear?"

Sena merely shrugs her shoulders, she continues to scrub a stain with unnecessary force.

Mary presses on. "You can confide in me, dear."

Sena meets Mary's gaze. "All my friends have departed. The Gem isn't the same. Many of the new girls are…" she hesitates, "…of *ill morals*."

Mary gives an empathetic nod. "You still have Frank and Spider, don't you?"

Sena exhales. "Frank? Which one—"

Mary smirks, "Frank Gates. Not my Frank. So, many Franks around the Gem, eh?" Sena and Mary share a small laugh.

Mary smiles. "See I knew there was some joy still inside of you."

Mary suggests, "Let's go inside and prepare costumes in the dressing area. The two engage conversation about daily life, the weather and upcoming shows.

"Yes, Frank Gates is more of an acquaintance than a friend. Spider—I think they may be of ill morals also."

Mary presses her lips thoughtfully and clasps both hands. "Spider is a good man at heart. Yes, he needs direction from time to time. I have taught him manners and conversation skills."

Sena whispers under her breath as she hangs up a costume. "I have doubts."

Mary bestows a few nuggets of wisdom. "Aiming high for moral standards is a must. There are many shades of gray. We all seek to fill a void, to grasp at joy where we can. Sometimes we err, but we must see past the errors of our ways and focus on the heart."

Sena continues to prepare for the show.

Mary pats Sena's shoulder before heading inside. Later, when Sena returns to her room, she finds a small vase on her dresser with a single carnation. A note from Mary next to the flowers:

*What lies in the heart is what matters most.*

Sena smiles, holding the note to her chest, inhaling the flower's faint scent.

**Letter to Sena from Milton Holter, Berkeley, California**

Dear Sena,

Father, Mother, and I were delighted to hear from you. So glad you are enjoying Missoula. We love living in Berkeley, though I miss our house in Helena. Mother has been unwell with a nasal drip but is on the mend.

Sending our love,

Milton

Days later, Mr. Pierce announces The Gem's temporary closure for lineup reorganization. Besides Sena and Spider, everyone has been dismissed or has departed on their own accord. Sena learns Frank Gates has departed for a theater in Billings. Sena wonders if her conversation with Mary led to these changes.

By evening, she joins the Pierces, Davenport, and Spider for dinner. Food was catered from a restaurant. Conversation buzzes about the upcoming auditions. Davenport's military friend was coming, as well as an associate of Pierce's from Texas. They were assembling an all-star cast for an all-new Gem Stock Company. They asks Sena and Spider for recommendations. Laughter and energy filled the room.

By the next day, Missoula was buzzing. The hotel next door was full of out-of-towners, performers came in droves, and The Gem's sudden increase in visitors was a topic of discussion among even their vaudeville rivals at the Exchange.

During auditions, Sheriff Prescott arrives unannounced. The room fell tense.

"Mind if I look around?" he asks, eyes sweeping over the room, suspicion etched in every line of his face.

Davenport folds his arms. "Do you have a warrant, Prescott?"

"You've got an awful lot of strangers in town," Sheriff Prescott says coolly.

Pierce steps forward, "We're bringing nothing but the best to Missoula. Now, if you've no other business, we have auditions to resume."

Sena's stomach knotted. Something about Prescott's presence felt like a bad omen.

That evening, Sena busies herself backstage, humming an old Swedish tune as she organizes costumes. Spider, passing by with a crate of bottles, stops short at the sound of her voice. Leaning against the wall, he watches her, a smirk playing at his lips. There was something sweet about her optimism, despite everything. She turned suddenly, startled, sending a box of hats tumbling to the floor.

Spider laughs, stepping forward. "Let me help."

They kneel together, hands brushing as they gather the hats. Looking up, Sena says, "Do your remember the night when Gloie and Maud were arrested? Mr. Pierce punched the bag of flour. Does he have angry outbursts often?"

Shrugging his shoulders, Spider says, "No. Wouldn't squash a fly. I'd rather he take his fists to flour than us! A man wronged must let his anger out somehow."

Then, without thinking, Spider leans close to Sena.

Heart racing, Sena remains frozen, not pulling away.

Heavy footsteps echo down the hall.

"Fresh biscuits and soup!" Davenport calls.

Spider was close enough to kiss her lips, yet he jerks back at Daveport's voice.

Awkwardly, they stand up, their skin brushing against one another a their arms. Sena clears her throat, "They're expecting us up front." She brushes her skirt downward and scurries away. Spider trodding behind her.

As she ladles soup, her hands tremble, thinking about the near miss of the kiss from Spider.

Davenport sets a parcel on the table. "Spider, this came for you today."

Sena raises a brow. "A parcel? Who from?"

Spider takes a sip of soup from his spoon, then stands to inspect the package. Looking down at the box, he pauses, tapping his fingers on the package. "Aye from me, sister. Likely some scrumptious treats."

Sena goes to bed restless, ruminating about the near miss of a kiss with Spider. She drifts off dreaming of him.

A sharp knock woke Sena.

"Sena, dear?" Mary Pierce's voice called from the hall. "Are you in there?"

Groggily, she slowly gets out of beg. She opens the door, rubbing the sleepy seeds from her eyes.

Mary and a maid rushes into Sena's room and begins to collect Sena's belongings. "Pack her bag. I'll help you." Mary speaks with urgency.

Sena blinks, still groggy. "What? Where am I going?"

Mary states matter-of-factly. "You'll be boarding with Frank and I for a while."

# Chapter 12

**May 1902, Missoula, Montana**

As the day slips by like shadows in the night, Sena's unease festers. She needs answers. Desperate, she rifles through the Pierce's house, searching for a newspaper.

She flips through the pages, her breath hitches, her eyes scan for any news as to why she's being forced to stay at the Pierce home. She hears Mary's footsteps, so Sena resumes making some tea in the kitchen.

"Good morning, Sena." Mary greets her.

Sena nods. "Good morning. Do you think I may be able to return to my room at The Gem soon?"

"No." Mary responds quickly and stern.

"What has happened?" Sena questions.

Mary slowly sits down at the kitchen table. "Have a seat."

Sena's eyes widen. She is confused and sits looking to Mary for direction.

Mary hesitates, which is unusual as she always has the correct words. "Spider—"

Sena interrupts Mary. "If this is about the kiss—"

Frank Pierce walks in to the kitchen eyes widened turning his head at both Mary and Sena. Remains silent.

Mary's eyes widen and she leans in and whispers, "What kiss?!"

"It was *almost* a kiss." Sena whispers back.

Frank clears his throat. "I am going to get my daily shave and meet with the attorney."

Mary and Sena nod and bid Frank farewell.

Mary returns to her normal tone. "This not about any kiss. Spider has been arrested."

Sena gasps in shock, "For what?"

"I am not aware of all the details. It is unsafe for you to stay at The Gem right now. There are some new pending laws. Davenport is traveling, and it is for the best for you to stay here for the time being."

A couple of days pass by. Sena zealously searches for answers by reading the newspapers. She finds some news articles. She learns Spider's real name—John Stett. She learns Spider's claim about the package Davenport had brought inside was not from his sister. An icy dread creeps through her veins. William Carlton, the insufferable gambler was involved. Sena thinks as she reads, *"Carlton must have drug Spider into this mess."* Reading between the lines, Sena sees it for what it is: a setup. Spider is a pawn, a convenient scapegoat in a dangerous game.

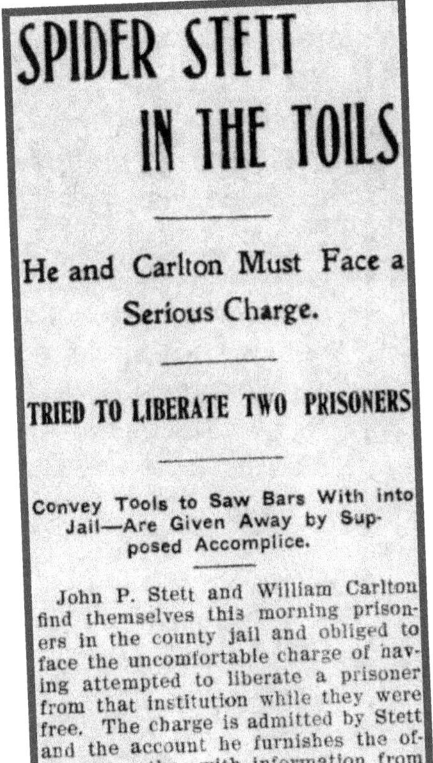

# SPIDER STETT IN THE TOILS

He and Carlton Must Face a Serious Charge.

### TRIED TO LIBERATE TWO PRISONERS

Convey Tools to Saw Bars With into Jail—Are Given Away by Supposed Accomplice.

John P. Stett and William Carlton find themselves this morning prisoners in the county jail and obliged to face the uncomfortable charge of having attempted to liberate a prisoner from that institution while they were free. The charge is admitted by Stett and the account he furnishes the officers together with information from other sources they have received characterize their attempt as a daring piece of work which only by rare good luck and the perfidy of a presumed friend was spoiled and George Kirkwood and Charles Fisher, prisoners at the jail to answer a charge of attempting to burglarize the Western Flouring company's mill office safe, are not now at large instead of prisoners.

The affair as learned from Sheriff Prescott's force and the county attorney seems more like fiction than a reality. Several days ago Stett was confined at the jail without the formality of a charge being made against him, it being done to assist his sobering up from a protracted spree. Carlton, his companion now in trouble, was also at that time a prisoner at the jail serving 30 days for a petty offense. The four were cellmates and became quite friendly. The first intimation of harm came to Sheriff Prescott in a communication from Sheriff Jack Conley of Anaconda, who with a letter of explanation enclosed a letter written by Kirkwood to an Anaconda man named James Berry. The letter to Berry was to the effect that "if you furnish three burrs to John P. Stett( care Gem Theatre, Missoula. I'll tip the dump." Sheriff Conley, to whom Berry had given the letter, was told that "burrs" meant steel files; and "tipping the dump," meant cutting out of jail. He communicated these facts to Sheriff Prescott. Being convinced that a bold attempt at jail delivery was intended, the officers proposed to carry the deal a little farther. They secured three metal files which were delivered to Stett at the concert hall. Yesterday morning Jailer Sloane found the tools at the jail window at a point on the sill where they could be reached from inside the bars as the window was opened. The arrest of Stett followed. He frankly admitted his connection with the matter so far as handling the files, went, incriminating Carlton

A man, known in Missoula as "B
Jim," or "Scar-neck Jim," was arr
ed shortly after the capture of K
wood and Fisher, at Moscow, Ida.
der for arrest came from Missoula
on receipt of information by Sh
Prescott that he was a pal of
prisoners in the **burglary**. Since
capture an attempt has been mad
secure a statement from the Miss
men that would warrant prosecu
further. This could not be obtai
and feeling that no good would
low further detention ,the Mos
prisoner was yesterday ordered
charged.

Information that came to Sh
Prescott last night has given ris
the theory that Stett was associ
with Kirkwood and Fisher prior
the attempted mill robbery, and
he could give an account of the af
that would reveal circumstances
now known. It is asserted that
men met at the Gem theatre wl
Stett was employed. The matte
being investigated.

She learns according to Spider did received the package, yet did not want to get involved, so he gave it to Carlton who carried out the instructions by smuggling the gold briars into the jail, a tool for Kirkwood's escape. The pieces fit together like a sinister puzzle. John Berry's letter did not identify Carlton at all. Spider was guilty by association. The newspaper details his sentencing—ninety days behind bars. Spider got off lightly, a fine of $25, with the option to work it off at $2 per day. But none of it sits right with her. She desperately wants to believe Spider is telling the truth. The air in the room suddenly feels too thick. Sena presses a hand to her chest. Her empathic heart feels for Spider, as he did not deserve this set up.

## October 1902, Missoula, Montana

The summer months passed in a blur for Sena. She remained with the Pierce family for a few weeks after Mrs. Pierce gave birth to her second daughter, Montana Fernella Pierce—whom they affectionately called Fern. Afterward, Sena returned to The Gem Theatre, rejoining the lively and ever-evolving cast.

The Gem was more than just a theater. It is a beacon of entertainment in the West, celebrated for its refinement, modern amenities and unwavering commitment to high-class performances. Newspapers praised it as one of the cleanest, coziest, and brightest theaters in the region—a place where audiences could enjoy top-tier entertainment without fear of anything unseemly or objectionable.

Sena thrived as part of The Gem Stock Company, the theater's resident troupe, performing in a rotating repertoire that kept audiences engaged week after week. Yet, The Gem was far from static. A steady stream of special acts arrived, ensuring fresh spectacles for eager patrons.

Each Monday brought a new playbill, featuring an exhilarating mix of comedy, opera, drama, burlesque, and high-class novelty acts. Acrobats defied gravity, comedians left the crowd roaring with laughter, and vocalists—like one particularly "wonderful cultured soprano"—filled the theater with breathtaking melodies.

Nightly, the curtain rises at 9 pm. Setting off a seamless succession of vaudeville acts that never allowed for a dull moment. Pierce and Davenport only book the most legitimate, first-class acts.

For Sena, the theater is more than a workplace. It has become a world of light, music, and motion, where every night brings a new story, a fresh thrill, and an audience eager for more.

In the dressing room, Sena removes her eye makeup, while

listening to the Italian harpist on stage. Lost in the music she jolts as a pair of hands cover her eyes.

A man's voice, "Guess who? I'm back?"

114 • *Jennifer Toelle*

listening to the Italian harpist on stage. Lost in the music she jolts as a pair of hands cover her eyes.

A man's voice, "Guess who? I'm back?"

# Chapter 13

**One week prior to the last scene in chapter 12:
October 1902, Butte, Montana**

Back in Butte, Sena's friend Lulu and a few settle in for an evening performance by a traveling stock company. To their astonishment, a familiar actor appears on stage. A ripple of gasps spread through the audience as they recognize him as, Owen Bockley!

After the gasps and sighs, Owen pauses. He reads the audiences shock. He pauses and announces, "Yes—it's me, Owen. I'm back in Butte .It was necessary for me to go undercover for a role. I've been performing under a different stage name in the eastern circuit.".

Lulu leaves her seat and picks up her pace to search for Owen backstage. When she finds him, she slaps him across the face. "You scoundrel! You think she waited for you? You abandoned her. You abandoned us!"

The actors backstage chuckle. Owen brushes off Lulu's anger as if it were nothing more than stage dramatics. Owen smiles with charm, "Where's my Sena at?"

"Not here. She's in Missoula!" Lulu says, arms crossed.

Lulu walks to her father's office at the theater. She takes out a piece of paper and starts writing a letter to Sena. It was crucial for Sena know of Owen's surprise return. Lulu writes to warn her.

## Missoula, Montana

Sena cheerfully gathers the day's post, delivering letters to the others before glancing at one addressed to her in Lulu's familiar hand. Tearing it open, she read the words once—then again. Disbelief stole the air from her lungs. The letter slips from her grasp.

Dear Sena,

I have frightful news! Owen has returned under the guise of another stage name. This has surprised us all! That scoundrel. How scandalous of him! He is asking for you. Please keep a steady guard on your heart.

All my best,
Lulu.

Davenport stands at the bar. He notices the letter fall. He strides over, picks it up, and glances at Sena's pale face.

"Owen?" he asks surprised. "You were married to Owen Bockley? *The comedian*, Owen Bockley?"

Sena's body tenses. She nods, barely able to move. With slow, trance-like steps, she turns and retreats to her room.

Mary is at the theater helping a duet rehearse. Sena's distress distracts her.  Mary retrieves the letter from Davenport, "How ever are you not aware of Sena's severed relationship with Owen? You know how gossip flutters around like butterflies."

"Well..." Davenport says as he places his hands on to his belt, "I knew Owen had left his wife high and dry. I was not aware it was *our Sena*. Are you certain?"

Mary sighs. "I must find Frank to inform him about this at once. We cannot have Owen showing up here at The Gem."

Sunday night fades into restless hours. The Gem's stage will be lit tomorrow, but Sena's mind is elsewhere—on Owen, on what she will say to him. Tears fall.

Later, Frank Pierce arrives at The Gem, Mrs. Pierce runs, ushers him into the side to discuss Sena. Others observe the interaction.

Mary lifts her skirt slightly on both sides as she ascends the stairs. Carrying herself gracefully, Mary follows the sound of the tears.

Mary knocks upon Sena's door softly, "Sena. It's Mary. Mary Pierce."

Sobbing continues to line hallway walls.

"Go away." Sena cries hysterically.

Mary opens the door, persistent to talk with Sena. Mrs. Pierce sat beside her, voice firm yet kind. "You mustn't go to Butte."

Sena is emotional. "What if he comes here?"

Mary claps Sena's hands in her own. "Sena, dear, we will protect you from him. You do have the divorce decree?"

Sena nods. "He never showed up in the courtroom to contest it. He may not even know we're divorced."

"Then write him a letter," Mrs. Pierce urges. "We'll send a copy of the decree. Mr. Pierce is traveling to Butte next week to scout talent—he can deliver it personally."

She pulls Sena into a brief embrace. "Erase him from your thoughts. He is the past. Write your letter, say what needs to be says, and focus on tomorrow's performance."

Sena buries her head in her hands. "I simply cannot perform. I'm..."

The following night, just before the show, Sena pressed a sealed letter. She handed it to Mr. Pierce before she went on.

He places a comforting hand on her shoulder. "I'll handle this. Now go sing your heart out."

After the show, there was an Italian harpist playing when Sena was backstage, listening to it while taking her eye makeup off. She jolted as someone's hands slid across her eyes, covering them. A man's voice, "Guess who's back?"

Sena's heart races as she turns around and sees Spider instead of Owen. She exhales in relief.

**While this historic fiction novel is told mostly from the lens of Sena's perspective. The following presents a snapshot of time from Frank Pierce's perspective.**

**January 1903, Missoula, Montana**

The acrid smell of the cigar permeates the air of The Gem's office. Pierce tallying the last of the business receipts. He closes a ledger. Overhears an exchange between Spider and Sena—her flirtatious laughter bouncing through the air. Pierce takes a puff of his cigar and stands up. Walking out, a concerned look on his face as he goes through the door, Sena is ascending the stairs to the overhead rooms as Spider is drying a stein. Spider glances over at Pierce, noticing his stern expression.

"What's crawled up your back?" Spider jokes.

"What are you doing with Sena?" Pierce questions.

"Huh?" Spider makes a confused face.

"Don't play games, John." Pierce shakes his head.

"Why are you so hot headed this evening?" Spider says as he folds a towel.

"You are leading her on. Or are you already ruining her name?" Frank presses.

"You think I? You think... me?" Spider points a finger at his chest.

"Are you being straight with me?" Pierce stares down Spider. "I heard her flirtatious laughter and you're teasing her."

Spider shrugs. "It's nothing out of the ordinary. Being kind to the ladies as you and I do 'round here everyday."

Pierce smiles. "Yes, we all love the ladies 'round here. There's a difference between treating them with affectionate kindness and respect and leading them astray." Pierce takes a puff of his cigar. "She's naïve. We have shielded her. You know from the vice that occurs from time to time. I'm trying my damnedest to make this variety theater top-notch!"

Spider laughs. "I remember when you cleaned house. Why did you kept the likes of me?"

"Because you, my boy, are a star at serving drinks. You are a fixture of The Gem!" Awkward silence lingers. "Be careful. You're apt to break her heart."

"Nah, she was married to that slick ass comedian Bockley. That lass ain't naïve."

"*She is naïve*—he deceived her. Don't you be deceiving her, too. Shall I remind you? YOU have a WIFE."

Spider scoffs, "Can you tell me where my wife is?"

"You haven't heard from her?" Pierce leans his back against the bar, crossing his arms.

"Nah, last I heard Coeur d'Alene or Spokane."

"This business can be hard on marriage bonds. I know quite well. Guess I got lucky, third time's a charm with my Mary."

"Aye! Mary is quite 'The Gem.' And she puts up with the likes of you!" Spider jabs.

They both chuckle as Davenport enters from the back of The Gem overhearing the last part of the conversation.

"Yes, siree. Marriage in show business is like gambling and you are already in debt. Don't know where Chloe is these days." He quickly changes the subject. "Say, you both read the papers today?"

Pierce nods. Spider shakes his head to the negative.

Davenport continues, "Sherriff Thompson's been tasks with trying to rally folks around ending gamblin' in Missoula County."

Spider laughs hard. "Here? End gamblin'? That will never happen." Looking over at Pierce. "Is that the real reason your knickers are tied?"

"Perhaps officials will come to their senses, license it like they do the alcohol." Davenport adds.

Pierce drops his elbow to the bar counter and rubs his forehead. "There's many people mounting against us. We are not a raunchy saloon. We are high-class entertainment here. During slow periods, alcohol and gambling revenue keep our business from failing. I suppose I gotta comply with anti-gambling rule. State law. If Sheriff Thompson is gonna enforce it?" Shaking his head and walking over to reach his coat and hat. "Goodnight, gentleman."

Outside the Pierce home, the late night chill gives Pierce goose bumps. He looks around scanning his surroundings closely. He quietly places his feet upon the few stairs to the porch and enters the front door, carefully taking off his hat and coat. After shedding his heavy coat, he still feels a great weight upon him.

Pierce ruminates his worries, *"Can my business survive if gambling is outlawed? The increasing support of prohibition, forbidding women to work... I need actresses. Will I still be able to provide for his family?"*

He quietly walks into the bedroom. At the foot of the bed, he removes his shoes. He leaves his overclothes on and climbs into the bed. He looks over at Mary sleeping peacefully. He takes his pocket watch out of his pocket looking at the late hour. He arches his back and gazes into the darkness of the ceiling.

The next morning, he wakes to the cries, coos, and babbles of his baby and toddler.

He hears Mary humming and singing, "Shhh, PaPa is sleeping."

He later enters the kitchen, Mary greets him, kisses him on the cheek, placing some toast and eggs in front of him. She sits down slowly and smiles at him with a glance he understands she's about to tell him something important.

"You will want to get used to these sounds, dear. We are about to have another." Mary smiles and strokes her stomach.

Pierce smiles, yet inside the weight of the city's politics weigh on his mind. He feels there is a storm a brewing against his livelihood and means to provide for his family.

Mary contends, "It would be in our best interest to hire a housekeeper and cook by summer's arrival."

"Yes, dear." Taking a bite of his toast. "I best be headed downtown for my daily shave.

His stride electrifies the sidewalk as his cane taps in step with him. He tips his hat and bidding a good day to those he meets along the sidewalk. Pierce takes a friendly approach to winning the city folk over. His aims to prove he is indeed a high-class citizen and he provides wholesome quality entertainment in his concert hall. As he walks, smiling and whistling along, he sees Sheriff Thompson and Mayor Smith, conversing. Pierce cheerfully greets people as he dodges this duo, determined to avoid them. He squeezes into the barber's chair just in time.

Good morning Mr. Pierce, "What's new at The Gem?"

"Ah, planning on bringing a brilliant shooting team, husband and wife duo to the entertainment lineup." Pierce says enthusiastically.

"Sure to draw a crowd." The barber adds. "The new mustache cup and shaving brush you requested has arrived."

As Pierce lies back in the barber's chair, he stares out the window onto the street. He observes Sheriff Thompson and Mayor Smith talk as the barber takes the blade finely shaving his chin.

**February 1903, Missoula, Montana**

Midmorning flurry of activity swirls around The Gem. Many prepare for the star national performers opening night.

"Where's Dave?" Pierce asks as Spider passes him in the hallway carrying a box to the front of The Gem.

"Haven't seen him. Probably with that new lass Minnie." Spider responds as he makes eyes at Sena who is coming from the opposite direction carrying a washboard and bucket of clothes towards the back of building.

Pierce shoots an unspoken warning glance at Spider not to flirt with Sena.

Mary passes by, walking to the prop room with a costume. "Must put the finishing touches on this costume for Miss Mexis. It was caught in a snag at her last performance."

"Oh, have they arrived?" Pierce asks.

Mary walks with a spring in her step gliding past her husband. She nods, "Yes. They are upstairs resting. And Frank, please place the advertisement for the housekeeper. Must be able to cook!"

Hartwell, Frank's son comes inside the back door of The Gem tossing a baseball.

"Hi Papa. I want to come watch the show tonight. I want to see these sharp shooters!"

"Heavens no! You can't be here at The Gem anyhow. You know they are cracking down on minors being here in the first place!."

*Hartwell Pierce.*

"C'mon, Pa!" In his Irish accent. "Please, Pa. I'll hide upstairs. No one will know I am here."

Davenport walks by interrupting his conversation with Hartwell. "Pierce, we have to get the gambling equipment up. They are gonna raid any day now. Now, where is..."

Pierce nods at Hartwell. "Okay, well be back here before the sun goes down."

More actresses and actors shuffle in all directions in the back hallway. Pierce left alone as everyone buzzes about. Shaking his head, walks to the back of The Gem, walks out the door to the alley, inhaling a deep breath of fresh air. It was an unusually warm day in February. He takes out a cigar. Sena stands outside, and begins to wash her clothes.

"It's a beautiful sunny day." Sena says, scrubbing her clothes against the washboard.

"Sure is." Pierce says taking a puff of his cigar. "Sure is." Obvious stress upon his face.

"Big act this evening." Sena attempts to make small talk. Pierce nods.

A prostitute passes them in the alley and she asks Sena for some lye soap. Sena ignores her and continues scrubbing. "I hear they are very popular. She shot above some royal's head."

Pierce grins and nods. "Yes, at an apple above the Venezuelan president, I believe."

He walks back inside and stops short, turning to look back at Sena. He takes notice of her hair pin with blue gems sparkling and reflecting in the sunlight. And then looks down the alley to see the prostitute is entering the back of a boarding house. He walks back inside and finds Mary working on the costume, and paces back and forth.

"Whatever is the matter, Frank?" Mary presses, "You are acting like you have never had a performance in here."

Pierce sits down, places his hand upon his head. "I'll tell you. Spider is about to make Sena a soiled dove. Dave is showing up late this week. He's not here yet. Must be in love again. And we have to cease gambling. Next, they are fixin' to take away our liquor sales. Mark my words!" His eyebrows furrow in anger and anxiety.

Mary's head leans to the side. "Calm down. You have fought and won before."

"No, Mary. This is different. Have you read the paper? Anti-gambling is state law. The new sheriff is fixin' to enforce it. This isn't a he says, she says case about morals and my operation here. And Mayor Smith…" takes another puff of the cigar.

Mary reassures him, "This act tonight is fixin' to bring in the masses—"

Pierce interrupts her, "We must block off the front. They are shooting real bullets at a damn glass ball. The pieces of glass are apt to injure someone or worse, kill—."

Mary ever so polite and mannered, "Yes, Davenport and the staff are setting up and taking precautions. These are experienced shooters. They have performed in almost every hall in the country."

Pierce, puffing his cigar. "This is an expensive act. What if they put a bullet in the walls?"

Mary looks at him, brushing off his comment. "And Minnie—Minnie is the name of Dave's new lady friend. He will be here before the show begins. He's never not shown by curtain call. Rumor is they are getting married. "

Pierce's eyes roll upward.

Mary continues. "And I will talk to Sena. I highly doubt she would become a soiled dove. She would be a lovely influence on Spider. Now, relax those shoulders, dear." Picking up the costume and gracefully putting a hand on her hip. "I must run along. Hartwell is waiting for me to return before the babies wake up from their nap. I promised him a new baseball bat today."

Pierce's eyes grow wide with concern, "Damn it, Hartwell!"

Mary tilts her head puzzled.

Pierce says, "Hartwell was here a few minutes ago. He's **NOT** at home with Missoula or Fern!"

"Oh heavens! I better rush home! I bet he has asks our neighbor to look after the girls." Walking out of the prop room and peeking her head back in, *"Do not forget to run the advertisement!"*

As the day turned to night, Pierce speaks with Spider at the main floor bar, then climbs the stairs to his post at the second-floor bar. Dave Kelsey takes his place to light the stage, and he sees it illuminate. The Gem Stock Company Players perform a few acts.

Pierce sweats profusely as Davenport steps upon the stage. Davenport extends his arms theatrically.

> *Now, what you all have been waiting for." Prepare for your blood to run cold as this amazing husband and wife team, are truly, Shooting Stars! People say Miss Mexis handles a rifle better than Buffalo Bill. Her husband William Coleman has the world's record in fast pistol shooting. When practicing last, he shot 700 times—685 of those hitting the bullseye! You've all heard about them shooting an apple overtop of Venezuelan president's head. Well, they don't use an apple. Tonight, you will see them use a glass ball the size of an apple. And when it shatters—prepare to be amazed!"*

Pierce's anxiety heightens while the show is going on, because the performers are shooting real bullets. He looks up at one moment to see Miss Mexis shoot at a cigar in her husband's mouth. He hears Mr. Coleman mentioning something about an Italian father and placing a breast plate as a target upon his wife's bosom, where he announces he will shoot 20 bullets at his wife!

As Pierce's nerves intensify, he asks one of his employees to take charge of the second floor bar so he can take a break. Going up, Pierce breathes slowly and deeply. The sound of shattering glass and repeated applause overwhelms him. He wanders into a room and realizes it is Spider's. He collapses in a hardback chair, wiping sweat off his forehead. Calming down, he spots a blue hairpin. The shiny hairpin on his side table prompted him to wonder about its presence. It looks identical to the one Sena was wearing earlier in the day.

# Chapter 14

**March 1903, Missoula, Montana**

Inside The Gem's office, Pierce and Davenport review lists of potential acts. Pointing at a photograph and poster, Davenport says, "People are recommending we book this act."

"Not in my theater. They are connected to the elitists. I won't stand for it," as Pierce refills cigars in his humidor.

"Perhaps it would bode well for those pushing for social reform?" Davenport suggests.

"And what? Bow to their anti-liquor sentiment? Saloons and variety theaters are our community hubs. People gather here for fellowship and camaraderie, not for taking a stake in a moral high ground. They are here to escape their reality, enjoy a good show, laugh a little." Pierce closes the humidor and gets up to get a ledger off a shelf. "Speaking of which are you planning to attend the Democratic primary and are you willing to be a delegate to the city convention? Tom from the Central Saloon inquired."

Davenport nods. "Yes…"

Pierce takes a puff of his cigar. "I'm planning to go to the city convention as well."

Silence lingers as they continue to look over the acts to book.

Davenport breaks the silence. "I reckon you are correct. I wish we could prove our value to the community and stamp out the naysayers. Hell, we just brought in a national act of sharp shooters that packed the house!"

Opening a ledger, "This anti-gambling law being enforced at the local level is cutting into profits. I've been thinking perhaps it's time to branch out and acquire a restaurant as well."

"Are you sure it's the best time to do this?" Davenport asks.

"Davy what are you getting at?" Pierce snaps.

Davenport pauses and speaks. "Everyone seems to think you are a tad more stressed per your usual. And you have another baby on the way."

Pierce says cooly. "I assure you, I have everything under control." Leaning back he adds, "Plus, the way I figure, local officials won't stop with gambling. They will come after liquor, too. Afraid the Garden City will be a dry town soon. We need revenue to keep the concert hall thriving. Some of these acts are requiring higher deposits to book well in advance." Pierce adds.

Mary busts into the office frantic holding her belly. "Frank are you okay?

"Of course dear, are you okay?" Pierce replies, confused by Mary's question.

"Well, I came as soon as I heard the news!" Mary shouts.
"News?" Pierce questions.

Davenport and Pierce look at her perplexed.

"You found the dead body in the Florence hotel?" Mary asks.

Pierce and Davenport shake their heads and speak in unison,
"No..."

Pierce chuckles, "You've misheard. Of course, murder is no
laughing matter, but **Prescott Pierce** found a dead body at the
**Missoula Hotel.** Good Lord Almighty! People are mixing up the
Pierce men again. It's fun having two sets of Pierce families
situated near or running hotels, eh?"

**May 1903, Missoula, Montana**

At the Pierce home, Frank enters the front parlor midday, he finds
Mary overcome with uncontrollable sobs. "What's happened?"

"Hartwell and I got into a horrid disagreement. His disrespectful
nature was appalling." Wiping her nose with a handkerchief and
then placing it back into the pocket of her dress.

"Where is he?" Pierce asks.

Shaking her head, "I do not know."

Pierce paces back and forth in the parlor room. Silence lingers for
several minutes.

Mary breathing deeply and changing the subject. "Have you placed
the advertisement? The baby will be here soon."

"No, Mary, I have not."
Pierce snaps.
Mary cries, again.

Sternly Pierce says, "I'll find Hartwell and I will place the advertisement." Pierce grabs his cane and walks out the door, closing it a bit too hard, yet not quite a slam.

*Note: $8 in 1903 would be $288.79 per week in 2025. In 1903, the average housekeeper/cook made approximately $2.50 to $5.00 per week. Most would receive lodging. Paying $8 per week is an above average wage.*

He enters the newspaper office. "I would like to place an advertisement. For a housekeeper, that must be able to cook well. Eight dollars per week plus lodging in the house. Ask for Mrs. Pierce."

He places some dollar bills on the clerk's desk and begins to exit.

The clerk looks up wide-eyed, "Eight dollars per week? Are you certain Mr. Pierce?"

"Indeed." He walks out of the newspaper office walking the city of Missoula aimlessly searching for his son.

Pierce is mentally and physically weary. He walks into the police headquarters and locks eyes with Chief Hollingsworth.

"Goodday, Pierce, are you coming to turn yourself in for something?" Chief Hollingsworth asks.

With a solemn, concerned expression and stressed tone, Pierce shakes his head, saying, "I need help to find my son, Hartwell."

Later that night, Pierce steps into the bedroom. Mary sits by an open window, a book resting in her lap. A soft breeze carries the scent of spring and the distant trill of birdsong.

She looks up. "Did you find him? I stayed up all night, worried when you didn't come back."

"Yes, Mary," Pierce says quietly. His face was solemn, his eyes heavy.

"Where is he? I only heard one set of footsteps."

Pierce hesitates. Then he blurts, "I had him arrested—for incorrigibility."

Mary's eyes fill. She turns away and presses the book to her chest.

"I know it's hard," Pierce says gently, "but I hope this will be a turning point for him. Prescott Pierce did the same with his Frank a couple of months ago. Had to send him to reform school in the end. I'm hoping it won't come to that. Tomorrow, Hartwell will face the judge. He'll promise to do better. I believe he will."

Mary bows her head and wipes her cheek. "I remember Prescott Pierce's Frank going to reform school. Folks kept asking me about Hartwell, mixing up the boys. It's hard with two Mary Pierce's in town."

She gives a sad, half-hearted smile. "You'd think they could tell the difference. Our boy's the one with the Irish lilt." Mary stands placing her book upon a shelf. "Have you sent word to Julia?"

Pierce avoids eye contact. "The police officers at the station will see to it she is notified."

"Should you not send word yourself?" Mary presses. "*She is his mother.*"

Avoiding Mary's remark, Pierce takes off his shoes. "I reckon I should sell the horse. I'll visit Marsh Stables tomorrow."

"Oh, Frank, you wouldn't sell the horse, would you?"

**June 1903, Missoula, Montana**

A warm breeze blows as Pierce walks out of the barbershop around noon. He sees Spider up ahead with a piece of paper in hand, who charges towards him in urgency. Pierce stops perched with his gold cane, looking down as the sunlight reflects upon the golden hues.

Spider hands over the paper with an angry expression.

"What's this?" Pierce unfolds the paper.

As Pierce reads, Spider vents his frustrations. "Red was arrested last week and now this? Is this legal? It's robbery and discrimination against our livelihood. I'm going to go talk to Yerrick about this! Somebody has to do something."

Pierce shakes his head, solemn expression. "Have you talked to Red or Tom?"

"Tom's reportedly furious about Red's ordeal. It's creating a bartender shortage because others are scared. They have up and quit." Spider says.

"Let's go pay Tom a visit over at the Central Saloon." Pierce says places a hand on Spider's shoulder with concern and whispers, "Act calm, and friendly to everyone we pass, you understand."

"Yes, sir." Spider sighs and drops his shoulders.

They continue walking, making small talk with people along the way and drum up business for their upcoming shows.

As they enter the Central Saloon, they see Tom, where a silent nod is exchanged by all. Tom extends an arm and head nod, leading them to his office. They discuss the paper where they are the target of liquor license fines. The accusation that their liquor license does not apply to multiple bars in one building. The City of Missoula is claiming that they need an additional license for every stationed bar in the building.

Pierce shakes his head. "I already pay for a liquor license and a variety hall license. That's over $500. They want me to pay for two more liquor licenses to operate in one building, and fine me!"

Tom nods. "And to boot, this absurd treatment of arresting Red for selling alcohol to a Native. They are making it harder for us to run our businesses."

"It's like we have a constant target on our backs," Pierce adds. "I'll gladly pay for my licenses, but if I'm not informed about needing additional ones, how can I be fined?"

They agree to see an attorney together to fight the fines. They also discuss political affairs.

"Well, gentleman, I must go fetch Hartwell, we are due in the courthouse soon," says Pierce.

"What business do you have there today?" asks Tom.

Pierce stands, his derby hat in hand. "I'm signing the commitment papers today to send him to reform school."

"Perhaps that's for the best. They're cracking down on minors loitering around places selling liquor." Tom says as he takes a drink. "Your little ones won't be affected as they are at home."

Pierce and Spider stay for awhile and continue to chat with Tom and his employees. On their walk back to The Gem, Pierce's cane taps the sidewalk rhythmically as they walk.

Spider vents his frustration, "I want to show these officials my fists!"

Pierce calmly advises, "A closed fist is the lock of heaven, and the open hand is the key of mercy."

Spider gives Pierce a sideways glance, "You preachin' at me?!"

"Nah, just impartin' my wisdom." Pierce smiles wide. "Ever tell you about the time I fed all the newsboys in Butte at Thanksgiving? Let me tell you some officials there did not like that much. My kindness, my open hand, changed public sentiment about treating those boys fairly. Far better impact that shoving my fists at someone. Pierce winks and looks up at The Gem's entrance.

# Chapter 15

**Continuing from Frank Pierce's perspective.**

**June 1903, Missoula, Montana**

The day had come for Hartwell to go to work on a farm instead of reform school. Hartwell wears a look of deep sadness and bewilderment and does not want to leave.

Mary looks Hartwell in the eyes as if he were her own son. The step mother status had no bearing on the love and care she provides. "Take good care of yourself." She embraces him snugly.

The warmth of the day seems to amplify the heavy sadness hanging over the Pierce family. Mary's hug was tight, her own chest constricting slightly with unshed tears, her heart aching with a physical pressure. Hartwell's shoulders slump under the weight of his promise, a tangible burden he carried. His face, usually flushed with youthful energy, was pale, the blood seemingly receding from his skin under the pressure of his anxiety. Even Pierce, outwardly stoic, shows the strain in the tightening of his jaw and the subtle tremor in his hands as he gripped his son's shoulder one last time before they turning leave.

"I promise I will be good and turn around my behavior." Hartwell says in his Irish inflection.

Emotions are high as Mary follows Frank and Hartwell to the porch. She watches as they walk away towards the carriage. Her heart breaks at this act of tough love.

## July 1903, Missoula, Montana

Summer settles in thick and slow, the kind that shimmered in the streets and clung to the skin. The heat is bothersome for Mary as she nears her due date. Thankfully, the new housekeeper manages the cooking which is easing some of the strain. Still, Mary gently suggests to Frank they hire Sena a few hours per week to help with routine tasks until things settle down.

Pierce agrees. He acknowledges Mary needs the support, especially with the long hours he works at The Gem.  And though he didn't say it outright, he hopes Sena's presence will keep her out of Spider's orbit, at least for now.

That morning, Sena descends the stairs from the rooms overhead, adjusted the buttons on her sleeve, and climbs into the waiting carriage where Pierce sat stiffly. They were barely underway when a man catches their attention. The man is running with a paper waving it in his hand, shouts "Pierce! Pierce, wait!"

Pierce exits the carriage. The man hands Pierce a telegram.

He unfolds it quickly. As his eyes scans the lines, his expression drains to stone. He leans into the carriage, voice tight.

Pierce wipes sweat from his brow, "Sena—go back inside, pack a few things. Just enough for a few nights. I have to leave town immediately. Mary could use the help… especially with the new baby coming."

Sena nods without a word. The gravity in his tone left no room for questions.

The ride to the Pierce home in South Missoula passes in near-total silence. Even the clip of the horse's hooves on the road seems to whisper, muffled by tension. It is the kind of silence you can hear settle between two people—a silence full of things unspoken. Pierce does not share why he is leaving town so suddenly.

When they arrive at the Pierce home, Frank speaks with Mary in hushed tones behind a closed door. Minutes later, he emerges, hat already in hand, and leaves without a backward glance.

Sena waits a beat before stepping softly into the parlor, where Mary is sunk into the edge of the settee, one hand resting on her pregnant belly.

"What's happened?" Sena asks gently.

Mary's voice trembles and wipes her sniffles with a handkerchief. "Hartwell's gone missing." Tears pour down her face. "He ran off from the farm he was sent to work on."

She presses her hand over her mouth. "Do they have any clues where Hartwell has gone?"

"No, I wonder if he's gone to find his mother, Julia," says Mary.

"Mother?" Sena asks.

"Yes, Hartwell's mother is an actress, Julia O'Neil. She once worked at The Gem. She is Frank's ex-wife." Mary explains.

Sena asks, "Is Julia Irish?"

Mary lets out a cathartic laugh as Sena's question brings some comic relief. Mary explains, "Yes, she is. Hartwell was born in Montana. Julia returned to Ireland when he was a small lad. He spent his formative years there. He returned to America just before Frank and I married.

Sena smiles as she says, "Oh, I see. Now, I understand."

Pierce was burning both ends of the candle, though he'd never admit it. The Model Restaurant was nearing its grand opening, and every waking hour seemed to be swallowed by contractors, menus, and finding decent linen that wasn't stained with the sins of a mining town. He told himself it was about legacy—about building something clean and respectable, something that might someday outshine the stories folks told about his family. But truth be told, it also helped to keep his mind off his concerns for Hartwell.

The reformers were growing louder, and the mayor louder still.

"That variety hall of yours— The Gem—" Mayor Smith had said just last week, while tipping his hat with mock civility, "might soon be a relic of a more reckless time. Missoula is growing up."

Behind the mayor stood Chief Hollingsworth, stiff-backed and eager to please.

"We're under direct orders," he'd added, "to rid this town of vice. Don't expect exceptions."

Pierce head nods, jaw tight.

Pierce thinks, *"Let them try. Let them come."*

Midsummer, Mary gives birth to a baby boy, Frank, Jr., given his father namesake. This new addition to the family makes Pierce realize the magnitude of what his is building. It's not just a concert hall. It's a secure future for his family.

Pierce is reviewing bills in his office at The Gem. The air hung heavy with smoke and the scent of warm whiskey spilled somewhere beneath the bar. The scent entices him to have a drink at the bar. After pouring a glass, he walks back towards the office. He hears a door creak open followed by the sound of Spider's footsteps and coughing. Something in Pierce's gut goes tight.

"Spider," Pierce calls, voice sharp. "Come down to the office."

As Pierce hears Spider's boots scuff the wood and his raspy cough, Pierce shakes his head prepping himself to have a serious conversation with Spider.

Once Spider enters the office, Pierce stands and walks over to close the door behind them. Pierce asks, "Were you in one of the ladies' rooms?"

Spider leans on the desk, pale and winded and quiet. He doesn't answer the question.

Pierce leans his elbows onto the table, cigar between his fingers. "Were you in Sena's room?"

Spider signs, "Yes, but it's not what you're thinkin.' The zipper caught on her dress. She couldn't reach it. I helped. Looked the other way while I did it, too."

Pierce's brow furrows. "Why not ask one of the other ladies?"

Spider shrugs, then winces. "She don't get on with any of 'em. Thinks they look down on her."

Pierce remains in silence staring at Spider. "I don't believe you."

Spider's jaw twitches. "You calling me a liar?"

"I'm saying I don't like what it looks like. Not in my place. Not after everything we have built here." Pierce says firmly.

Spider annoyed rolls his eyes, "And, you can't do this with out me. I entertain customers while I bartend. I'll do what I damn please."

Pierce points with his cigar, "You keep your hands off her. I promised her *you* would keep her from frisky customers after Curly died."

Something flickers in Spiders eyes. He blinks repeatedly. "So this is about Curly," he says, voice hoarse, "You watching over her 'cause of him? Why?"

Pierce's hand curls into a fist against the desk, then relaxes.

"Yes," he admits. "Because of Curly. He looked out for her when no one else did back in her Butte days. She was just a kid, Spider. And because I'm not about to let the city call The Gem a brothel. I'm trying to build something better—higher class. You understand that?"

Spider rubs at his eyes, his voice raw. Points to his chest, offended. "You think that of me? That I'd pay her for services? Hell, Pierce, I had plans with Curly, too. We were gonna open a place—our own saloon. Right before he died, we even had the papers started." He sniffs hard. "I ain't been right since. That was the last time I got blind drunk. Dust in my eyes, maybe, but I still see him sometimes when I walk by the river."

Pierce softens, just slightly. He nods toward the handkerchief still clutched in Spider's hand.

"You need to see a doctor. That cough sounds like it's gotten worse."

Spider gave a half-hearted laugh. "You care about me now, eh? Don't worry, boss. Ain't dying just yet."

"Good," Pierce says, reaching for his ledger again. "Because we've got work to do. The city wants to shut us down. We're going to give them a reason not to. Even if they take away the liquor, you'll be a damned fine entertaining waiter!

## August 1903, Missoula, Montana

Sena steps through the back door of the Pierce home, her shawl clinging damply to her shoulders, the brown paper sack in her arms crumpled from the weight of goods inside. The scent of dried sage and sweet tobacco wafts faintly from the sack, but it isn't enough to mask the sharp sting of tears still fresh on her cheeks.

At the kitchen table, Mary and Pierce look up mid-conversation, their faces drawn and shadowed by the weight of weeks of worry. Legal papers scatter across their table like confetti after a grim parade.
Mary's softly says, "They want you behind bars, Frank. They won't stop until they bleed us out or drag The Gem into the gutter."

Pierce rubs his temples, his lips pulled tight. "I built that place from brick and breath—"

Sena pauses in the doorway, trembling.

Mary notices first. "Sena, what's happened?" Her tone shifts from weary to motherly in a heartbeat. "You look pale as the moon."

Pierce rose to his feet, his voice suddenly sharp. "Did Spider—did he lay a hand on you?"

Sena shook her head violently, barely able to speak. "No. No, nothing like that. Davenport to fetch the doctor…"

She chokes on her words, then spills them out:

"Spider's burning up with fever—don't think he's going to make it."

Pierce's chair scrapes across the wood as he stands. "Mary, I'm going." He turns to Sena, already grabbing his coat. "I'll get the carriage hitched. Sena come back to The Gem with me. He will want you there."

*Historically inspired digital rendering of
John "Spider" Stett. Historic narratives describe
Spider as resembling 1930s actor, Clark Gable.*

# "SPIDER" IS DEAD
## HIS FUNERAL TO-DAY

Missoula, Aug. 25.—John Stett, known widely as "Spider," a sobriquet which he earned several years ago, when he appeared occasionally in the fistic arena, died at 4 o'clock this morning at his rooms over the Gem theater. Stett was ill for about four weeks with pneumonia. Deceased was 35 years of age, a native of Ireland, and had been a resident of Missoula for about 15 years. He had been employed for several years in the Gem variety hall, and was quite extensively known from his connection with the place. The Eagles will have charge of the funeral, which will take place to-morrow afternoon from the Eagles' hall.

## September 1903, Missoula, Montana

A packed courtroom is tense, supporters of both sides. Sunlight slants through the long windows, catching the gold on the seal of the State of Montana above Judge Hayes head. The reformers sat in one row like buzzards dressed in their Sunday best. On the other side sat Mary, pale but composed, holding baby Frank Jr. in her lap, and Sena beside her, hands clenched tight.

Pierce stands at the defense table with his attorneys Marshall and Stiff. Judge Woody presides. The witnesses list for the defense is solid. Spider was their star witness. Since he died, it leaves a hole for the defense.

County Attorney Hall delivers his opening remarks, "Your Honor," he begins:

> *this case is not about personal reputation— It is about the law. The statute reads clearly—any person who employs or  permits women to sing, dance, or exhibit themselves in a place where spirituous liquors are sold is in violation. The Gem is a variety hall in name only—it is, in effect, a saloon with a stage. That is illegal.*

Pierce's jaw flexing, but he says nothing.

Police Chief Hollingsworth is called to the stand. He raises his right hand, swore in, and took the stand with stiff authority. "On the evening of August 12, I entered The Gem by the front entrance," Hollingsworth says, eyes narrowing. "There was a bar in front and a performance in the rear theater. A connecting door was open. Liquor was served to both men and women."

Prosecutor Hall leans in. "Did you see women on the stage?"

"Yes, sir. Dancing and singing, responds Chief Hollingsworth.

"Was there any disorder?" Prosecutor Hall questions.

"Not that night." Chief Hollingsworth explains.

The defense took over. Attorney Marshall stands, slowly buttoning his coat. "Chief, you've also visited the other saloons and theaters this month, have you not?"

"Yes." Chief Hollingsworth answers.

"Did you observe dancing and liquor sales at those establishments?" Attorney Marshall asks.

"Objection—irrelevant," the Prosecutor Hall snaps.

"Overruled," Judge Hayes says, not even looking up. "Answer the question, Chief."

Hollingsworth gritted his teeth. "Yes."

Marshall turns slightly toward the jury. "Yet you only swore out a complaint against The Gem. Why?"

"Because The Gem is... more visible. More egregious."

"Or more *successful*?" Marshall says coolly.

The defense calls Ed Martin, the undersheriff who testifies, "I was present the night in question, but the Gem was conducted in an orderly fashion and abides by the rule of law. Cleaner than most places, in fact. I've had less trouble there than any other saloon in Missoula."

"Any minors present?" Marshall asks.

"No, sir." Martin replies. A stir passes through the courtroom.

Then comes Mildred, a slender woman in an embroidered shirtwaist and with too much rouge. She sits tall in the witness chair, chin high.

"State your name and occupation." Prosecutor Hall says.

"I decline to answer on the grounds it may incriminate me," Mildred says.

"Were you employed at the Gem?"

"Same answer, sir."

Davenport is called to testify, He wipes his spectacles before answering.

"Are you the manager of the Gem?"

"Yes, sir," Davenport replies.

"Were women employed there on August 16?"

"Objection," Marshall says quickly. "Mr. Davenport is within his rights not to answer under state privilege."

"He may decline," Judge Hayes allows.

"I decline to answer," Davenport says firmly.

The jury deliberates for only two hours.

When they filed back in, the room stood still. The foreman, a balding man with ink-stained fingers, stood and clears his throat. "We, the jury, find the defendant, Mr. Frank Pierce... not guilty."

Gasps echo in the courtroom for both sides. Pierce exhales for the first time in days. Mary clasps her hands to her lips in relief. Pierce glances at Sena across the room. A moment of victory, there was something lost too. Spider was gone. The Gem would go on. But not unchanged.

# Chapter 16

**Back to Sena's perspective
September 1903, Missoula, Montana**

Sena's world is gloomy. As Sena gazes into her own eyes, the weight of survival bears down heavily on her. Each brushstroke through her hair feels like a silent acknowledgment of the lives lost, a solemn tribute to the memories she carries within her. The quiet solitude of her vanity mirrors the somber stillness of her world, a place where shadows linger long after the light has faded. Yet, in the depths of her gaze, a faint glimmer of resilience flickers. Placing her brush down, she strides over to her satchel removing her diary. She strikes a match to light a candle. The flickering candlelight casts a warm glow over the room as she opens her diary to a fresh page. With a sense of purpose, she dips her pen tip into the inkwell, ready to capture the swirling thoughts and emotions that dance within her mind. The scratch of the pen against the paper breaks the silence. A therapeutic act of pouring her soul onto the blank pages. Each stroke feels like a release, a cathartic unraveling of the tangled threads of her innermost thoughts. The candle flame seems to dance in rhythm with the flow of her words, creating a sanctuary of introspection.

Diary Entry, September 13, 1903

Death has plagued me this past year and a half. First it was Curly, then Mr. Yerrick's young daughter, Zetta. The last death came this past month. It was the worst death of them all. I shall never recover! My whole-body aches from his death—Spider. Oh, Spider, I miss you. The world is so cruel!

I am stirring and steeping some Yellow's Lady Slipper tea to calm my nerves. I have become very anxious all the time. Upon physician's advice, alternating this tea with the Valerian root tea is an excellent remedy. The tea is tastier when I pour in a bit of milk.

Zetta's death hurt the entire community of Missoula. The song sung at her funeral echoes in my mind: Lead Kindly Light. The smell of the flowers, what an abundance of flowers. Zetta and her parents had journeyed to Michigan and Portland. Better physicians there, to treat her ailments. Better altitude for her heart sickness. It's so sad, nothing could heal her. The city people here say it was the longest funeral procession to her grave the city has ever seen. Carriages dripping with flowers. Her friends in multitude showed up to pay their respects. Goodness, golly, I hope when my time comes, there are hundreds of flowers.

     I think about death a lot. So many, too young, passing on. It makes me question God. Those who had never met Zetta, like me, attended the funeral to support Mr. Yerrick. I don't know him well, but felt obliged to go — he must be a good man. After all, he bailed Spider from jail, not making him suffer.

How God could be so cruel to us on earth? Taking a young, lovely woman and allowing her to die. Her doctor wrote a letter of sympathy, which was published in the newspaper.

I have clipped it because the words so beautiful, finding some solace from the pain, the best portion was,

"…in youth we cling to life. We are terrified at the very thought of personal dissolution. The youthful tenacity of life is like a green apple that clings to the branch, and cannot be plucked thence except by breaking the twig on which it grows; old age on the other hand has lost its strong attachment to life; it is like the ripe apple in autumn; you touch it and gently and it drops freely into your hand… To sleep; perchance to dream; aye, there's the rub, yet Bright things never die, Even though they fade."

Weekly Missoulian May 8, 1903.

My grief gnaws at me, a raw ache deep in my gut. I miss them so much it hurts, a pain shared by all of us left behind. Who is this God, to take them away so young? It's not fair to us mortals on this earth.

Spider was truly a gem of The Gem. A quiet strength stood behind the bar, cleaning glasses and wiping away everyone's sorrows. He listened without judgment, his hands steady as he polished each glass, erasing the streaks from our souls. He knew everyone's secrets, every bit of business. Why, why did he have to get pneumonia?

Trustworthy and dashing. His Irish brogue was unlike any I'd heard before, tinged with a British or Scottish tone. It was both sweet and gruff, a mix that made me fond of him. But when he drank, it was a slippery slope. He was a good man, and the drink made him fight, always defending those he cared about. I can still hear him saying, "Sena, my lass, I may be daft, but I have enough gold in my heart to fill this stein." Tipple, his dog, is now cared for by Davenport.

His death has wrecked us all!

Each night, 9pm magic swirls in taking hold of everyone in The Gem Theatre. Leaving the grief in a closed bottle for the night. Everyone a bit lighter, a bit jollier, content. A place where souls are nourished with hearty laughs and whimsical tales leaped from the stage. The Pierce and Davenport duo leaders in entertainment. They book the best acts. Excellence—they expect nothing but excellence, alluring flair to draw crowds and entertain with first-class performers. The Gem Stock Company crew forbade sadness. It was a feeling we had to suppress. Pierce would not have it during any performance—sadness multiplied sadness. Joy was the antidote—It was what we were indoctrinated to believe.

As long as joy swept over The Gem, we were to be swept up in a land where reverie reigns.

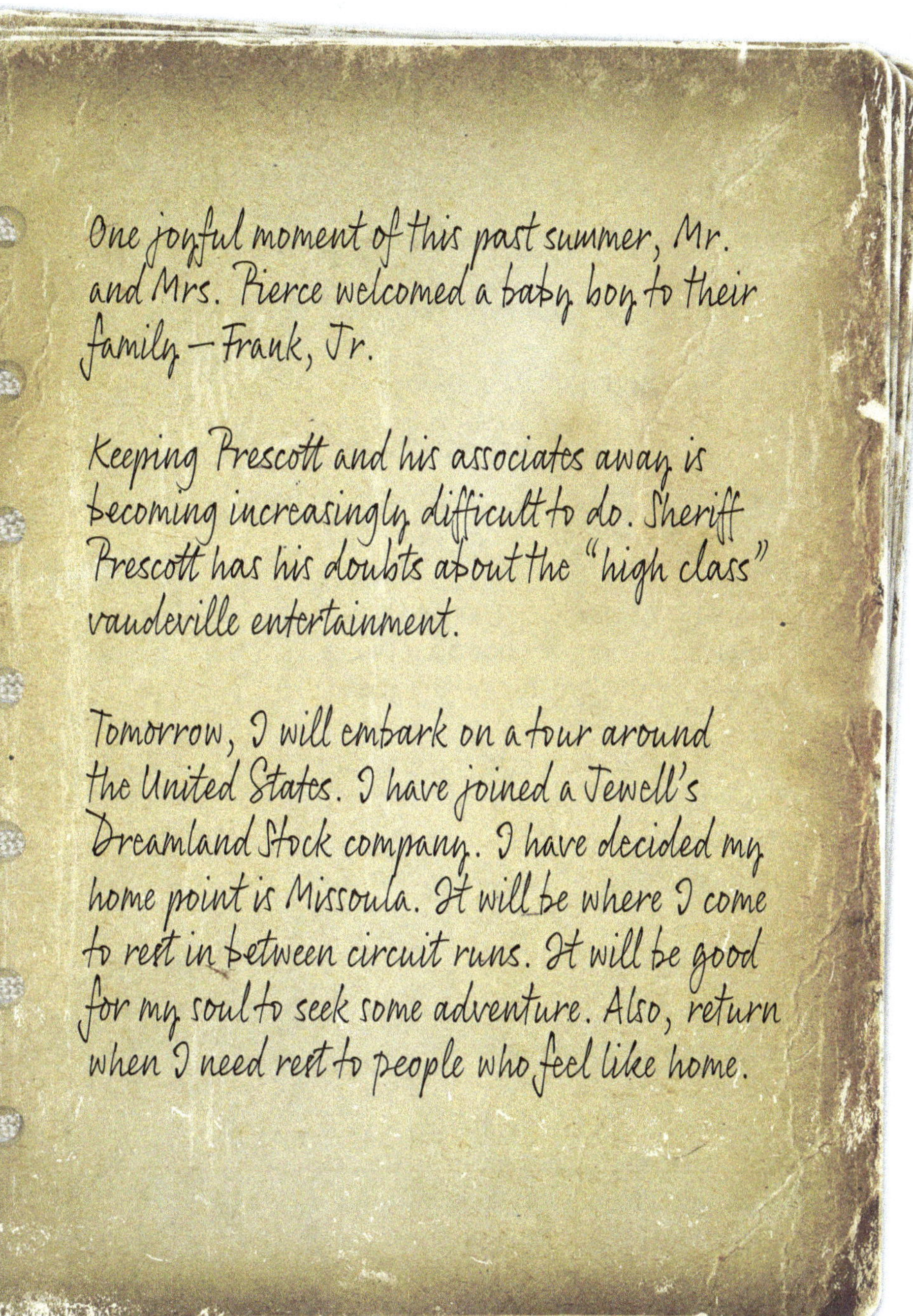

One joyful moment of this past summer, Mr. and Mrs. Pierce welcomed a baby boy to their family—Frank, Jr.

Keeping Prescott and his associates away is becoming increasingly difficult to do. Sheriff Prescott has his doubts about the "high class" vaudeville entertainment.

Tomorrow, I will embark on a tour around the United States. I have joined a Jewell's Dreamland Stock company. I have decided my home point is Missoula. It will be where I come to rest in between circuit runs. It will be good for my soul to seek some adventure. Also, return when I need rest to people who feel like home.

## Lead Kindly Light, by John Henry Newman, 1833

This hymn, sung at Zetta Yerrick's funeral was particularly beloved by those seeking comfort and guidance, including travelers, soldiers, and those facing uncertain times. It was sung by passengers on the Titanic

*Lead, kindly Light, amid th' encircling gloom,*
*Lead Thou me on!*
*The night is dark, and I am far from home,*
*Lead Thou me on!*
*Keep Thou my feet; I do not ask to see*
*The distant scene—one step enough for me.*
*I was not ever thus, nor prayed that Thou*
*Shouldst lead me on;*
*I loved to choose and see my path, but now*
*Lead Thou me on!*
*I loved the garish day, and, spite of fears,*
*Pride ruled my will: remember not past years.*
*So long Thy power hath blest me, sure it still*
*Will lead me on,*
*O'er moor and fen, o'er crag and torrent, till*
*The night is gone;*
*And with the morn those angel faces smile,*
*Which I have loved long since, and lost awhile.*

## Sena travels

Sena departs to tour with Jewell's Dreamland Stock Company. The Pierce's connections secure her a spot with this vaudeville tour. This decision comes as the law prevents females from working where alcohol is sold. Many Montana variety theaters and concert halls struggle with the daily operations and contemplate ceasing liquor sales.

**May 1904, Houston, Texas; Letter to Frank and Mary Pierce:**

Dear Frank & Mary,

It has been a most remarkable time here! The cast of the Jewell Dreamland Stock Company has come together like glue, and joy abounds among us. Alvido & Lasserre run a grand show here in Houston, with a most astonishing variety of acts. The crowds are lively, their applause heartier than any I have yet known.

Oh, what a delight it was traveling to Corpus Christi and Galveston. As I stood on the sandy shore, the salty sea breeze caressed my skin. I dipped my toes into the cool ocean water, feeling the gentle tug of the waves. Some seaweed and debris caught between by toes. Heavens! I didn't mind. The sound of the waves crashing against the shore is a soothing melody. I watched as seagulls cried out overhead. I gathered shells and bits of coral, their rough textures and intricate patterns. The sea wind danced around me, whipping the waves up and over, creating such a glorious sight—I could watch again and again!

How is Davenport holding up since his stroke? It was nice of you all at The Gem to rally around him. I crossed paths with an actress that was there for the benefit performance. Cannot remember her name, she says it was grand!

Mary,

How are the little ones? I expect young Frank is thriving by now. When I return, I shall have some new songs to sing for you. I have had the honor of understudying the great Zeta Lovell and, much to my delight, have even learned to mimic her British accent! You will surely have a laugh when you hear it. I crossed paths with Gloie and Frank Carroll twice!

I narrowly missed seeing Owen in San Antonio, arriving at the theater only a week after his performance. I learned he has moved eastward with his own company—the Bockley Stock Players. I shall have to take care to steer clear. My indebtedness to you both for helping me so, sever the ties to him.

I found a fine lavender bow in a millinery shop for Missy and shall keep an eye out for little treasures for little Fern and young Frank.

My circuit will keep me on the road for several months yet, but I expect to be back in Missoula by Christmastime.

With all my fondest regards,

Sena

## Summer 1904, Texas Coast

Summer of 1904 on the Texas coastline finds Sena lost in her inner thoughts. As she watches the waves rolling in and swirling backward in a gentle rocking motion, she bends down to pick up a coiled shell. She contemplates the idea that once a creature lived inside it, perhaps a whelk, a squishy creature that had obviously abandoned this shell for another. Wrapping her fingers around the shell, she wonders about the creature's decision to leave its protective home. This moment of reflection leads Sena to ponder deeper questions - why do creatures, including humans, run away from certain situations? Is it instinct? Is there a natural inclination to seek new horizons, like the whelk that ventured out of its shell? She recalls Aunt Lisa's words about her mother, how mother was always on the move, never sitting still for long. Sena draws a parallel between her mother's restlessness and the whelk's departure from its shell, realizing that perhaps we all have moments where we need to shed the protective layers of our lives in pursuit of new opportunities.

# Chapter 17

1904 to 1905, Sena travels Vaudeville Circuit across the Western half of the United States.

Jewell's Dreamland
Stock Players

Featuring

Sena Bjork
Cleo Samayoa
Zeta Lovell
Many MORE

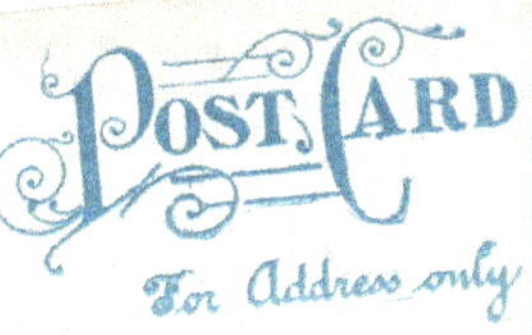

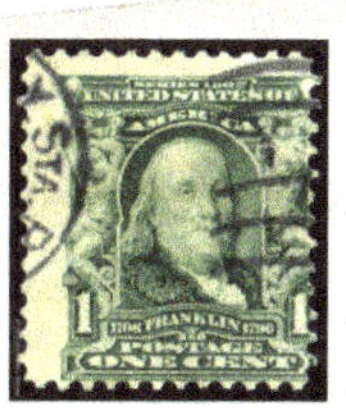

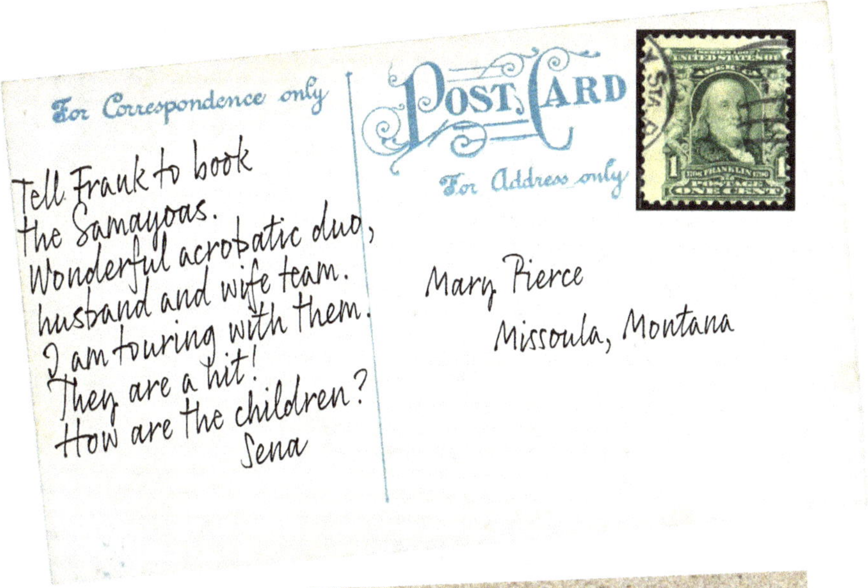
For Correspondence only
POST CARD
For Address only
Tell Frank to book
the Samayoas.
Wonderful acrobatic duo,
husband and wife team.
I am touring with them.
They are a hit!
How are the children?
Sena
Mary Pierce
Missoula, Montana

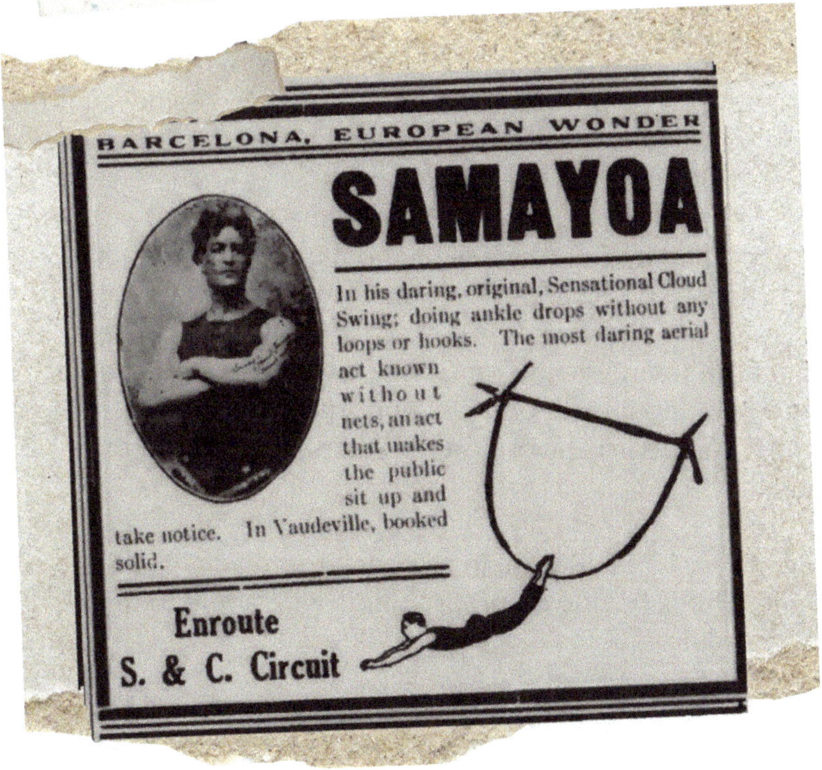
BARCELONA, EUROPEAN WONDER
SAMAYOA
In his daring, original, Sensational Cloud Swing; doing ankle drops without any loops or hooks. The most daring aerial act known without nets, an act that makes the public sit up and take notice. In Vaudeville, booked solid.
Enroute
S. & C. Circuit

## December 1904, Missoula, Montana

Gracefully grabbing hold of the handle at the depot, Sena exits the train and steps onto to the station platform, slightly lifting her skirt so that it does not get caught as she steps down. The sun is shining upon the chilly air. Her first stop is The Gem to get settled. She is planning to stay through the New Year as Jewell's Dreamland Stocky Company is taking a break for the holidays. She figures she can perform at The Gem if the law allows.

As her carriage arrives at The Gem, Dave Kelsey, the electrician greeted her. She finds it odd Davenport is greeting her at the front entrance; she heard Davenport had taken ill earlier in the year after a stroke.

Kelsey, "Hiya, Sena! Mary is in the back room fiddling with a costume. She is having some problems with some feathers." He says, chuckling.

Sena smiles and walks towards the back of The Gem to the dressing rooms. Peeking her head around the corner she sees Mary struggle with some blue feathers on a costume. "Don't let those feathers ruffle you!"

Mary jumps and laughs, "Sena!" Mary plops the costume down and walks over to Sena giving her a hug. "How was your ride in?"

"Admittedly, bumpy." Sena shakes her head.

"I'm glad you are here. Please help me with these feathers. I am due back at home soon. The children are expecting me to not take long this afternoon." Mary says, frustrated.

"Of course," Sena says, taking off her gloves and sitting down at a dressing table. "How is Davenport?"

Mary's somber look says it all. "He's declining. Stubborn. He does not want to admit he's ill. Frank is searching for replacements to help manage The Gem. Leaning towards Ashley Basco, but Basco's been focused on that theatrical troupe at the World's Fair."

"Oh!" Sena's eyes widened. "I'm sure Basco would be a great fit."

Mary tilts her head and raises a brow. "Yes, and Basco has been our stage manager from time to time."

"It's quiet here today." Sena sits awkwardly looking around.

"Hmm. Yea, we have a light line up this month. Frank is engaged in some meetings. There was a robbery in a safe downtown. Many stock certificates were stolen including one of Frank's."

"Oh, heavens!" Sena says as she adheres the last feather.

"Yes," Mary picks up another feather,  "and no one can quite fill Spider's shoes at the bar. Grief has consumed us all. Frank wants a bartender to perform like Spider did, and those are hard to come by. He also wants us females back on stage. My male persona act is a bit rusty." Mary laughs.

Dave Kelsey pops by the doorway carrying a case of liquor, "Mary I'm heading down to the Louvre to deliver this case to George."

Mary waves, feather in hand, "Okay, remember do not bring up Anna."

Kelsey nods and exits, "Wasn't planning on it."

"Is something wrong with Anna?" Sena asks.

Marys eyes widen, "Anna has filed for divorce from George. It's very messy. Anna has been staying at the Missoula Hotel. It's best not to take sides. The newspaper reports say she's asking for a steep amount in alimony."

"Oh, what a shame! It was such a beautiful wedding," Sena says.

"Divinely beautiful! And that wedding brought you to us." Mary applies the last feather. "Well, settle in. Glad to have you back for a while. Will you do me a favor? Take this medicine up to Davenport and see to it that he takes it." Mary half smiles.

Sena nods.

As Mary departs from The Gem, Sena ascends the stairs toward The Gem's overhead rooms. This visit she is assigned her old room from when she initially came to The Gem with the Kennisons. Opening the door, whiffs of pine, cedar, alcohol and musky cologne hit Sena's nose. Unglamorous, minimal and plain in comparison to the stage and grandeur below. Sena's fingers lingered on the pulls of the vanity. The air in the room seemed to whisper Spider's name, evoking a bittersweet ache in her heart. As she gazed at the familiar surroundings of her old room, a sense of nostalgia washed over her, bringing back echoes of laughter and whispered secrets. Despite Spider's physical absence, his presence lingers like a shadow, a silent companion in the overhead rooms. Sena closes her eyes, savoring Spider's ghostly embrace.

She unpacks a few things and goes to prepare some tea. Then finds Davenport's room. She yells out softly his nicknames, "Davy. *Dabby*. Davenport."

"Sena? In here." Davenport replies in his thick Boston inflection.

"Ja, Coming," Sena says carrying a tray into his room and sitting it on a side table.

"Knew it had to be you, I know that voice and inflection when you call me Dabby." Davenport grins looking at her. "Oh, Mary has sent you with that dreaded elixir!" he groans.

"Yes. You really must take it." Sena insists. "I was given instructions to see to it."

Davenport sighs, "You have better things to do than look after this ailing old man."

"You are not old nor a bother." Sena hands him his teacup and saucer and sits down on a chair near Davenport's bedside. "I admire your talent, Davy."

"Flattery, eh? I see your tricks, Sena."

They both laugh. Davenport gets choked up from the laugh. "I'm not the spry actor I once was. I wonder sometimes if I wasn't an actor, what would I have become? You are still young, you can still change course, Miss Sena. Perhaps you become a nurse?"

Sena smiles demurely as she helps him adjust his pillow behind his back. "Perhaps I am enjoying touring the circuit. I saw the ocean, sand, and seashells in Texas. It was heavenly!"

Davenport offers a slight smile. "Don't end up alone, you hear? So many of us in this business end up alone in the end."

"Mercy, you are not alone. You have all of us at The Gem." Sena insists. "And isn't there a Mrs. Davenport?"

"Chloe? She's not here." Davenport coughing. "When I had my first stroke. Wired her in the east. It took a great while to track her down. She showed up for the benefit show for my medical debts. She's mad for vaudeville. Chloe needs adventure. I am a fool for thinking she'd settle down at one theater."

*"Oh Dabby.* Ja have your Gem family. Your Eagles brothers, too."

Davenport grins and speaks in a theatrical voice and gestures wide. "No family but our show business family."

Sena sat with him as he told her stories of years gone by actors and follies, his days in the Civil War. She held him in great esteem for his talent and storied career. As he nods off to sleep, Sena pulls a soft blanket over him noticing his blue frail eyelids slumber. As she begins to exit the room, she meets Frank Pierce in the hallway.

"Well, hello Sena. How is our 'old man'?"

"I was successful in getting him to take his medicine. He told me war stories. Dabby is dire shape, should you wire Chloe?"

Pierce grimaces, "Chloe's in a contract with a burlesque circuit. He wouldn't want her to break her contract for him."

A look of concern washes over Sena's face. "He seems so sad."

Pierce looks disheartened and discouraged. He leans over and places a hand on Sena's shoulder. "Davenport would say, the show must go on, my dear." Deflecting the sad moment. "Well, I presume you had a long day of travel, sweetheart." Placing his arm around her shoulders.

Sena nods with tiring eyes, "Yes, I shall go lie down for a spell."

Pierce half bows, takes out his cigar and taps his cane. "Rest up, doll."

Sena slept through the afternoon. Her body was suffering from the train ride and travels. Rising, she splashed water on her face in the basin. She went to check if Davenport needed food. Upon opening the door, she found that he had left.

Maybe he is feeling better, she muses. Downstairs, she finds Dave Kelsey tinkering with the light sconces. "Have you seen Davenport recently?"

"I haven't seen him, no." Dave Kelsey responds.

Confused, Sena walks downtown. Being quite hungry, she enters the closest restaurant. Upon opening the door, she sees Davenport collapse. A collective gasp fills the restaurant. Uncontrollable spill into the street. A person eating in the restaurant goes get a doctor. Sena panics at the sight of Davenport's still body. It is a shock to see the powerful man she met only two years prior frail and lying on the ground.

Davenport is rushed to his room at The Gem, and prompt medical attention is given by Dr. Brown. While waiting for an update, Sena and others gather around a table in the concert hall. Dave Kelsey fidgets by tapping his fingers. Pierce tapping his gold cane. Her shock starts to subside. Dr. Brown descends the stairs at The Gem, his silence speaks volumes. The air was heavy, almost 10 times heavier than when they lost Curly or Spider. The realization The Gem had lost their 'Davy'—their theatrical genius, their Civil War hero, their Bostonian transplant, William H. Davenport.

## William H. Davenport's Funeral, December 18, 1904

Inside the Missoula Elks Hall grief and reverence hang heavy in the air at the funeral. Mourners with somber faces and tear-streaked cheeks of the mourners. The weight of loss seemed to press down on the shoulders of each person present. Their sorrow reflect in the slow, measured steps as they make their way to pay their final respects.

The Missoula Band's music wraps around the people gathering like a comforting embrace. It offers solace and a sense of unity in their shared grief. Heartfelt tributes sung by the men resonate through the hall, their voices trembling with emotion as they honor the memory of Davenport.

The procession to the cemetery is a solemn affair, the carriages move in slow procession as the mourners follow in quiet contemplation. The mile and a half journey feels like a symbolic passage, a physical manifestation of the emotional distance they now face without Davenport's presence.

Each flower that drapes the carriage carries not just floral offerings, but also collective love and memories shared by those who had known and respected Davenport. The finality of laying him to rest as a Civil War veteran adds a layer of historical significance to the proceedings, underscoring the depth of his impact and the legacy he has left behind.

## January 1905, Missoula, Montana

The new year brought promises of new opportunities as she resumes her place on the vaudeville circuit. Excitement bubbles within her as the spotlight beckoned, casting its magical allure on the stage where she belonged. Rehearsing tirelessly, she feels the thrill of anticipation building with each step closer to her grand return. The scent of the theater, the echo of applause—all whispered promises of a dazzling future awaiting her in the limelight of the vaudeville world. She was taunted with new desires. Her mind wanders at the possibility of being paired with any man onstage or in the audience at any moment. The stage boosts her self-confidence and makes her feel alluring and luxurious. She does not wait for the applause, she begins to crave it so much she makes it herself. A drastic change from the girl who was introduced to theater five years ago.

She struggles with caring what the Women's Christian Temperance Union would say about her lifestyle and occasional drinking. She aligns her belief of suffrage and equality. She disagrees about the alcohol. Alcohol consumption is intertwined with her profession. She often thinks, *"How can I be a liberated female, yet not be able to work where I want to?"*

---

According to the *Houston Post*, Cleo Samayoa divorces Manuel Samayoa in Beaumont, Texas on January 1905. Both are still touring vaudeville concert halls and theaters across the country.

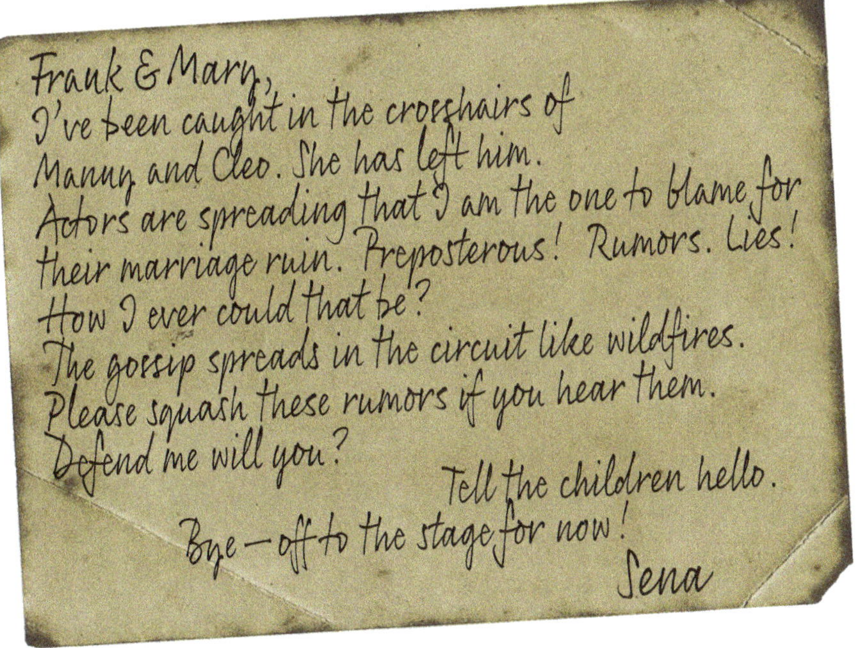

## Vaudeville's Struggle for Respectability: Navigating Stigma and Changing Perceptions

Vaudeville was on the rise, but in many places across the West, stage performers—especially women—were often associated with liquor, vice, and questionable morality. While a growing movement sought to establish vaudeville as wholesome family entertainment, the transition was slow and met with resistance. Performers like Sena found themselves caught in the shifting tides of public perception. Some recognized them as legitimate entertainers, professionals in their craft. Others, however, viewed both the performers and their audiences with disdain, unable—or unwilling—to separate them from the lingering stigma of the stage.

# Chapter 18

**August 1905, The Gem, Missoula, Montana**

The glow of the stage glares in Sena's eyes as she exits the stage. Her feet roll across the floor, springy, full of life and zest. She smiles at her fellow stage crew and entertainers as she goes backstage to gather her belongings. She moves with the light and carefree grace of someone who feels completely at home, as if the The Gem belongs to her. With rouge and cloth purse in hand, she hears Frank Pierce calling her name.

"Sena, a man is waiting out front, asking for you. Says he is a detective. Needs to ask you some questions. Prolly, nothing, sweetheart." In his calming Southern voice, Frank Pierce reassures her that there was nothing to fret.

In a confident stride, Sena gracefully walks to the front entrance of The Gem. Her eyes fixated on a passerby outside the entrance. She nods, acknowledging the detective. She extends an arm and slinks downward into a chair at a table near the bar. The detective follows her lead, sitting in a chair nearby and pulling out a small notebook and short pencil.

The detective begins expressionless, "Hello, Miss. I am Detective

Motts. I am here to speak to you about your mother. She has died under mysterious circumstances. I suspect foul play. I am investigating."

The detective spoke, his words sharp as a needle popping an inflated balloon. Sena's joy, symbolized by a balloon, escaped into the air. She cried, her body tensing with each tear.

Employees of The Gem notice Sena's distress. "Go find Pierce!" one of them shouts.

Detective Motts' relentless questioning doesn't give Sena a chance to recover or express her grief over her mother's passing.

Frank Pierce rushes in, "I think this is enough questions for today."

Motts continues, "Really, I must ask her more questions."

Turning his head towards Sena, "Did your mother respond to your letters?"

Dropping her head, staring into her lap. "No, sir."

Pierce insists, "This will be all you ask her. I will call for our sheriff immediately!"

Awkward silence persists.

Motts raises an eyebrow, "That won't be necessary. I have already visited the jail today. Spoke with your kind sheriff. I am to report back to them about your establishment." Motts continues his questions. "Please share with me where I may be able to find your father, Chris Leutner."

Pierce sits down to join them at the table.

"Christie? He is not my father." Sena sniffles. Pierce hands Sena a hanky.

Motts presses. "Where can I find your father?"

"I do not know. I have not seen him since I was a small child in Sweden." Sena's cries in between words.

Motts jots down some notes. "So, Chris is your stepfather."
Sena blurts. "No."

Detective Motts scratches his head and draws a line in his notebook. "Wasn't your mother married to Chris?"

Wiping her nose, Sena responds. "No. She was married to Chris' brother Henry."

Motts follows up. "Ok, where can I find Henry?"

Sena speaks in a muffled tone. "Helena. Works for Reinig's Store."

Motts follows up. "What was your mother's relationship with Chris?"

Sena explains, pausing her cries. "After my mother and Henry divorced, my mother lived in Butte with Christie. They were in an unwed union."

"Oh, I see. Your mother's boarding proprietor says your mother left several children in Montana."

Sena nods. "I have three sisters in Helena. Henry is their father. I have sisters in Sweden, too."

Detective, "No other siblings that you are aware of?"

Sena shakes her head.

"Do you know of a man by the name of Perry?"

"An actor, not sure if it's his stage name. My mother left Butte with him for San Francisco."

"Okay, thank you Miss Sena. Is there anything else you should share with me?

Silence.

Motts stares at Sena. "Who would want to hurt your mother?"

Sena's eyes alternate to focus as she begins hyperventilating.

Pierce leans down while telling the bartender to bring over a glass of water. Pierce says, "Let's breathe in and out, in and out."

Sena mumbles, "Henry."

Detective Motts, "Henry? – Your stepfather?"

Sena nods.

Pierce, concerned, looks Sena in the eyes and grabs her hand. "Look at me and breathe. Did your step father hurt you?"

Sena starts crying uncontrollably.

Pierce looks over at Detective Motts. "I think you have your answer." Looking back at Sena, "Breathe in and out."

"Very well, then." Detective Motts hands a card to them. "The county coroner's office in San Francisco has already made internment arrangements. Contact them about services." Tearing a piece of paper from his notebook, "Here is the name of the boarding house proprietor where your mother resided. I presume you will want at her meager belongings. Good day."

As Detective Motts exits, Pierce turned towards Sena, "Sweetheart, why don't you go lie down. I'll call for the carriage to bring Mary to look in on you later today."

Sena nods and walks frightfully to her room.

Pierce went over to the bar grabbing his cane. His grasps and releases the top of the cane over and over. Wiping a glass, the bartender asks Pierce, "Where did you learn to breathe in and out like that?"

Pierce's tense face "Childhood. I've witnessed some heinous things in my lifetime."

Sena steps into the dimly lit telegraph office, the sharp scent of ink and oil mingling in the air. The rhythmic clatter of a Morse key tapping out messages hum like a pulse against the quiet. She fills out the necessary slips, pressing the pencil firmly against the paper, as if the weight of her grief could be eased by the act of writing.

First, a message to the San Francisco Coroner's Office—formal, precise. Next, a note to her Aunt Lisa in Sweden, her handwriting wavering slightly at the thought of sending such terrible news across the ocean. Then to Cici Maley, her former caretaker in the Holter household. Finally, she indulges a whim, scratching out a short telegram to her old schoolmate, Marie. She had not been as diligent in writing as she had once promised.

"Stop apologizing for time lost," she scolds herself. "Just write." The telegraph staff glance at her as he mumbles to herself. With her last telegram sent, she stepped outside, the heavy door shutting with a dull thunk behind her. The weight in her chest did not lift.

## August 1905, Helena, Montana

The train ride from Missoula to Helena took nearly five hours, winding through Montana's rugged landscape. The rhythm of the wheels against the tracks is steady but unrelenting, like the ticking of a clock counting down toward something inevitable.
Sena sits near the window; her face reflected in the glass as the world blurred past. The mountains loom in the distance, dark and brooding against the afternoon sky. Anxiety twisting her gut, battling with sorrow. She has lost her mother—but really she lost her long before death. The idea of returning to Helena, to the place that had once felt like home, was bittersweet. Would it still feel that way? By the time she arrived, dusk had settled over the city in a soft, violet glow. She stepped off the train, her body aching from the journey.

Sena hops upon the trolley, the familiar clang of its bell and the jostling of passengers stirring memories from years past. As she nears Cici's print shop, her heart pounds. Would she even recognize me after five years have passed?

When she steps inside, Cici is wiping ink from her hands. The older woman looked up, her expression shifting from surprise to warmth. She lets out an unmistakable Irish greeting.

"Ah, Sena, my girl! Well, would you look at you—come here, love." She leaps forward to Cici, wrapping her arms around her, tears spilling down her cheeks.

Cici held her tight. "I received your telegram. My condolences." By evening, Cici prepares a comforting meal—stew, fresh bread, and warm tea—but Sena could hardly eat. Her appetite had been stolen by grief, her mother's death weighing heavy on her chest. Even the simplest notion—that Annalie had been taken too soon— was unbearable. But the deeper, unspoken truth, the suspicion of murder, clawed at the edges of her thoughts.

As the kettle whistles, Cici places two cups of tea on the table and looks at her thoughtfully.

"I'm glad you came here, Sena, but why my house and not the Sanderlins'?"

Sena shrugs, tracing a finger along the rim of her cup. "You remind me of home—the Holter's home. And I can't go there... they are in California."

A knowing smile spreads across Cici's face. "Well, a piece of news that might dry a tear or two, by gollies—the Holters are in Helena for a visit."

Sena's heart leapt. Relief flickers inside her, only to be quickly replaced by exhaustion.

"Whatever is the matter, dear, besides your mother's passin'?" Cici's voice was gentle, but Sena flinched at the question.

She hesitates, then sighs. "I'm a divorced woman of shame."

Cici waves her hand dismissively. "The Holters care for you Sena, not your circumstance. You shall go see them tomorrow, eh?"

Sena nods. Maybe seeing them would bring her some sense of peace.

The next morning, as she and Cici walks toward Rodney Street, Sena's stomach churns. The grief weighing on her was momentarily replaced by something else—a deep, unshakable sense of homecoming.

She knocks on the door, her hands trembling. A domestic servant answers, and from inside, a familiar voice rang out.

"Who's there?" Emily Holter's voice carried from the parlor, and as she stepped into view, her face lit up. "Oh, my—Sena! What a lovely surprise! Come, come in, my dear."

Cici steps in behind her.

"Oh, Miss Maley! Come, come. Sit."

But Sena couldn't hold it in any longer. She burst into tears, her sobs shaking her small frame.

Emily rushes to her side, embracing her. "Oh, what has you in such a state of distress, my dear?"

Sena swallows hard. "My mother has died."

Emily exchanges a glance with Cici—one full of unspoken words. Emily turns to her maid. "Go find Mr. Holter and Milton at once."

Soon, Martin Holter enters, Milton following a step behind. Milton's long frame now filling the archway. Vanished is the boy he once was running through the house tossing the baseball in the air.

"Whatever has happened?" Martin asks, his brow furrows. "Sena?"

Sitting down with them in the parlor, she pours out everything—her mother's sudden passing, the suspicions surrounding her death, and the detective from San Francisco.

Martin listens intently, his expression grave. Then, with quiet certainty, he says, "We'll go with you. You shouldn't face this alone." Then pausing and stroking his beard. "Wait..." a perplexing look, "where is your husband, Sena?"

Sena lets out a shaky breath. Shame overcame her as she shares the embarrassing details.

Martin and Milton grow visibly angry. Emily had a grievous look of concern. They all sat in silence for a few minutes, sitting with the shock of the news.

Martin stands up pacing the room and sighs. "You did what you had to do to restore your dignity."

His support floods her with relief.

**Montana Club, Helena, Montana**

That evening, Martin Holter enters the Montana Club, spotting Mike Reinig, owner of Reinig's Store is seated, a cigar resting between his fingers. Without preamble, Martin sinks into the chair beside him.

"How's Henry Leutner?" Martin blurts.

Mike arches a brow. "Well, hello, Martin! Good day to you." He took a leisurely puff.

Martin exhales sharply. "Apologies. Hello, Mike."

Mike chuckles. "Now, Henry... in trouble, is he?"

Martin leans forward. "Why do you say that?"

Mike's smirk fades. "A detective from San Francisco came by my store this morning, asking about him. Wanted to know about his habits, his travels."

Martin stiffens. "Has Henry traveled as of late?"

Mike nods. "Took a holiday about a month ago. Didn't say where.

Something about securing land."
Martin frowns and wonders. Did Henry know about Annalie's death? Did he—could he—have had a hand in it?
He sits down his high-ball glass. "Do you think Henry would allow his daughters to accompany my family to travel to San Francisco?"

Mike lets out a low chuckle. "I'd have a court order in hand if I were you. Henry may have you arrested for kid-snatchin'."

Martin sighs. "Will he be at the store tomorrow?"

Mike tips his cigar. "He's there now, stocking and completing the inventory.

## Reinig's Store, Helena, Montana

The glow of the outdoor lamps cast over the darkness of Helena's streets. The bell above the door jingles as Martin steps into Mike Reinig's store. The scent of tobacco and oiled wood fills the store, mingling with the faint hint of fresh ink from the ledgers stacked behind the counter.

Henry is behind the counter, sleeves rolled up, ledger open, but his expression shifts the moment he sees Martin approach. He stiffens, his hand gripping the edge of the counter as if bracing himself.

"Martin," he greets coolly. "To what do I owe the pleasure?"

Martin speaks quickly. "I need to talk to you about Annalie."

Henry's jaw tightens, but he keeps his tone even. "Tragic business." He glances at the cigar box near the till and lifted the lid absently, as if the conversation bored him.

Martin presses, "So, you do know what has happened?"
Henry says, "Some San Fran gent came round asking questions about Annalie."

Martin nods. "Your girls deserve to know. And they deserve to say goodbye."

Henry shut the cigar box with a snap. "They'll do just fine right here. No need to drag them across the country to bury a woman who never gave a damn about them."

"What choice did Annalie have? You battered her. Neither of you have custody nor fit to raise your children," Martin lectures. Martin's voice remained level, but there was a sharp edge beneath it. "They still deserve the to know and say goodbye to their mother."

Henry scoffs, crossing his arms. "You come in here, uninvited, and think you can tell me how to raise *my* daughters?" Henry continues with contention in his voice. "Just like you told Annalie how to raise Sena."

"I think you're trying to keep them from the truth," Martin counters. Henry's eyes flash with fury. "And what truth would that be?"

Martin leans in slightly, lowering his voice. "The detective from San Francisco has been asking about you."

Henry's fingers flex against his arm. "I told that detective all I know. How immoral that wife of mine was."

"He seems interested in your travels of late. Took a holiday, didn't you?" Martin says.

Henry let out a low chuckle. "If you think I had a hand in Annalie's death, Martin, you're even dumber than you look."

Martin's stare did not waiver. "Then let your daughters go to the funeral."

Henry exhales sharply through his nose, shaking his head. "Absolutely not. No one will show up a funeral for her."

Martin sighs. He had expected this, but he had hoped—*hoped*—that some part of Henry would relent. Awkward silence prevails. Henry with his back towards Martin as he stocks a shelf turns around and lifts his head and touches his chin. "All right. You can tell them. I won't stop that. But they stay put at St. Vincent's." It was the only ground Henry was willing to give. And Martin, knowing better than to push further, had to take it.

## St. Vincent's Academy, Helena, Montana

Sena's hands trembled as she stepped through the iron gate of St. Vincent's Academy. The afternoon sun slanted through the trees, casting long, dappled shadows on the playground where children laughed and ran.

She sees them immediately—Emma, Carah, and Edie—her half-sisters. Emma, the oldest, stood with a book tucked under her arm, her auburn hair catching the light. Carah and Edie sat on a bench, swinging their legs.

As Sena approaches Emma looks up first. "Sena?"

At the sound of her name, Carah and Edie turned, their faces breaking into smiles.

"Sena!" Edie squeals, scrambling off the bench and running into her arms.

Sena hugs her tightly, then glances at Emma, whose smile falters. "Why are you here?"

Sena swallows, kneeling slightly, so they were at eye level. "I needed to see you. There's something I have to tell you."

Emma's smile fades completely. "It's about our mother, isn't it?" Sena nods, her throat tightening. "She... she passed away."

Silence stretches between them, thick and uncertain.

Edie blinks up at her. "Like, gone?"

Sena nods again. "Yes, sweetheart. Gone."

Carah, usually the quiet one, wrapped her arms around herself. "Did it hurt?"

Sena hesitates. "No, darling. It was quick.
That was the first lie.

Emma, sharp as ever, studied her. "How?"

Sena forces herself to meet her gaze. "An accident."

That was the second lie.

Emma motions the sign of the cross and whispers, "In the name of the Father, Son and Holy Spirit." Emma looks up and softly says "we must pray for her, for her soul."

Sena's chest aches. "Yes. Yes, we should."

They sit in grief together a bond only they know having experienced life with their complex mother.

The train groans as it leaves Helena's depot, steam billowing into the evening sky. Inside the cabin, the rhythmic rocking and the occasional lurch of the cars made conversation sparse.
Sena sits next to Emily Holter, who occasionally pats her hand, offering wordless comfort. Across from them, Martin Holter read the paper, his brow furrows, while Milton stares out the window. The train was no luxury. Wooden seats made their backs ache, and the endless rattling wore on their nerves. The thin mattress in the sleeping car barely provides little relief. The constant motion, the whistle's sharp cries, the scent of coal and metal—it was exhausting.

Occasionally, they spoke.

"You doing all right?" Milton asks at one point, his voice gentle.

Sena manages a small smile. "I will be."

Emily sighs, stretching slightly. "They need to improve these trains. My back is going to be ruined by the time we reach California."

Martin chuckles. "You'll live, dear."

Emily shoots him a look but doesn't argue.

As the night deepens, Sena rests her head against the window, exhaustion finally overtaking her. The train barrels forward, carrying her toward the final, painful goodbye.

## August 1905, San Francisco, California

Sena's mother's boarding house in San Francisco is a narrow, aging structure with peeling paint and a faint smell of salt from the bay. The landlady, a stout woman with shrewd eyes, leads them up a narrow staircase. "Didn't know much about her," she says, unlocking the door. "Kept to herself. Bit secretive, if you ask me. She did say she left a lot of children behind in Montana."

Sena thinks to herself, "and she left children in Sweden, too."

The door creaks open, revealing a small, sparse room. A bed, a writing desk, a trunk.

The landlady points to the trunk. "I had the doorman bring down the trunk from the storage room. She was paying to have it stored. Still late with the rent most months. A man came by and paid her rent this past month—paid it through the end of the year. Well, leave you all to it."

Emily immediately began gathering belongings, but something about the room unsettled Sena. It felt... off.

Martin moves to the desk, shuffling through papers. "Letters," he mutters, unfolding one.

Sena reaches for the trunk at the foot of the bed. The one the landlady had pulled from the attic. She lifts the lid—and freezes.

Inside, under neatly folded clothes, were a few of stacks of letters bound with a black ribbon. She picked them up, her fingers trembling.

The first stack contains letters Sena had written to her mother when she was a small child still in Sweden. What was the reason for her not replying to my letters? She thought.

The next stack appears to be from random people Sena was not familiar with, yet the third stack—the name on the top letter made her blood run cold.

"H. Leutner."

Sena's breath hitches. "Henry."

Martin's head snaps up. "What?"

She hands him the letters. "These were written to Henry."

A thick silence fills the room. Emily stops folding a blanket. Milton's brow furrows.

"Why would your mother be writing to Henry?" Emily asks slowly.

Martin flips through the pages, his frown deepening. "These may be copies of letters."

***Taking a letter from the ribbon, Martin reads aloud...***
"Henry, I know what you did. You think I won't speak, but I will. You will not take what is mine."

Sena's stomach churns. "What was he trying to take?"

Martin's jaw tightens. He thinks internally, *Land*—He continues reading the page. "We need to take these to Detective Motts."

An eerie chill crept through the room.

## St. Boniface Catholic Church, San Francisco, California

The heavy scent of incense and fresh-cut lupine flowers filled the air inside St. Boniface Catholic Church, their sweetness mingling with the faint traces of melted wax and old wood. Candles flickered along the altar; their flames unsteady in the dim light. The organ's solemn chords swelled through the vaulted ceiling, echoing against the stone walls.

Sena sat between Emily and Martin Holter, her hands folded tightly in her lap. Milton sat at the end of the pew; his usual straightforward manner replaced by a stiff solemnity. None of them spoke.

The priest's voice, steady and practiced, filled the sanctuary. "Into your hands, O Lord, we commend your servant Annalie…"

Sena's throat is raw, unshed tears making swallowing difficult. She had spent her life at a distance from her mother—sometimes by choice, sometimes by force—but now, that distance was eternal. The finality of it settled like a stone in her chest.

The Catholic customs are foreign to Sena, because she attended the Lutheran church in Sweden. Her mother converted to Catholicism when she married Henry Leutner, a German Catholic. Her sisters are at a Catholic boarding school, St. Vincent's Academy. A Catholic service is what her mother would have wanted, or so she thought.

From the corner of her eye, she caught a figure standing near the back of the church. Detective Motts.

He wasn't mourning. He was watching.

The funeral mass continued, but Motts' attention was elsewhere. His sharp eyes scanned the pews, lingering on certain faces—men who bowed their heads a little too quickly, women who clutched their rosaries a little too tightly. He wasn't interested in the prayers. He was waiting for movement.

Motts joins Sena and the Holter's in a pew.

A man in a dark suit near the side aisle rose quietly, his steps careful as he slipped toward the rear of the church. A moment later, another followed. Then a woman. Each one making their way toward the confessional booths lined against the back wall.

Motts tenses. He watches as the first man disappears behind the heavy curtain, the wooden door clicking shut. The others wait, their heads turn.

Martin, noticing the detective's gaze, leansover slightly. "What is it?" He murmurs.

Motts kept his eyes forward. "The confessional. People looking to cleanse their souls after a sudden death? That's when you start asking questions."

Emily's grip tightens on Sena's hand. "You think someone here knows something?"

Motts exhales slowly. "I think someone here has a secret."

The funeral mass ends, and the priest gives the final blessing. "May Annalie's soul rest in peace."

But for Sena, peace was nowhere to be found.

As the they rose to leave, Motts lingers near the back of the church. The line for the confessional had grown. The detective's sharp gaze follows each person step inside, already piecing together the next part of the puzzle.

They all travel to the grave-site. Annalie had already been buried by the County. A basic plot, no frills, yet no longer a Jane Doe. She was not a nobody. She was somebody to Sena.  The San Francisco fog embraces them and the graveyard. The case wasn't closed.

# Chapter 19

**September 1905, Deadwood, South Dakota**

S ena steps upon the train platform in Deadwood. The cool September air wraps around her like a whisper of the past. The depot bustling with movement, but her gaze locks in on a man in the crowd. A familiar face—tall, broad-shouldered, with sandy blonde hair and piercing eyes that squinted just so. Familiar, yet who was he?

As he strides toward her with confidence, she reeled in her memory banks and recalled seeing him four years prior. She sees him at an Eagles benefit show while spending Christmas with the Kennison sisters.

"Good day," he says, removing his hat. "I feel as though we have met before."

Sena tilts her head slightly. "Perhaps. I travel quite a bit—I'm an actress on the vaudeville circuit."

"I'm Digby," he offers, his voice smooth and sure. "And you are?"

"Sena?" Looking around and pulling out a mother-of-pearl fan. "My name is Sena."

Digby's lips curled into a slight smile. "A pleasure, Sena. Will you be staying in Deadwood for long?"

"For a few months. I will be performing at the Green Front Theatre."

"Well then," he says, eyes twinkling, "perhaps I'll have to catch a show."

Before Sena could reply, an older woman bustles toward them. "Now, Digby, we'll be late for our departure."

Digby gave a polite nod. "Good day, Miss Sena. Perhaps I'll see you upon my return."

As he walked away, Sena finds herself breathless. There is something about the way he carries himself, the way his voice curls around her name. She had performed in countless towns, seen faces come and go, but this man—he was something else.

Sena settled into life at the Franklin Hotel, a grand establishment boasting modern luxuries—steam heat, an elevator, electric lights, even telephones in the rooms. The wide entrance pillars gave it a cosmopolitan air, and she relished the luxury of living there. Her evenings at the Green Front Theatre were filled with laughter and applause, and during the day, she played piano in the hotel's parlor, an arrangement that helped defer her costs.

One evening, as her fingers danced over the piano keys, she sensed a familiar presence. Looking up, her eyes met Digby's. He was leaning against the doorway, watching her intently.

"You play beautifully," he says, stepping closer to the piano. "Would you allow me to take you to dinner? I'd love to hear more about your travels as an actress."

She hesitates a moment, then smiles. "I'd like that."

Over the following week, their dinners turned into strolls through Deadwood's winding streets, the connection between them deepened, but Digby remains vague about his own affairs, and Sena, swept up in the romance, chose not to press.

The Green Front Theatre was a packed house with many acts including the famed pugilist, John L. Sullivan. Sena performed at that night. After the show Digby arrives at the stage door with flowers in hand for Sena. "You were enchanting," he murmurs, walking her back to the Franklin.

The dimly lit street filled with the scuffling sounds of hooves and carriages. The cool evening air carries the smell and swirl of dust. Her heart races as she feels his body's warmth with her arms locked in his. His rugged scent of sweat lingers in the air, mixing with the earthy smell of the city. Unlocking his arm, he leans in to kiss her. Her body falls backwards against the smooth texture of the pillar in front of the hotel.

As he pulls away, Sena touches her lips as she is smitten with him. Digby asks, "I shall see you later this week after your performance?"

Entering the mercantile store, the clerk greets Sena. While touching different fabrics, she hears women gossiping nearby. The first woman, "Well, that's utterly absurd! My son would ever associate with an actress!"

The second woman responds. "I saw him kissing her outside the Franklin Hotel."

The first woman gasps, "Nonsense! My Digby would never court a loose actress."

The second woman declares, "I assure you Mrs. Randaldt, this is what I saw as my carriage passed by last night. It may have been dusk, but was Digby and an actress from the Green Theatre."
Mrs. Randaldt's eyes closed in disbelief. "Oh, I must put a stop to this. His saloon business is tolerable, it is Deadwood after all. But never an actress. I shall put a stop to this at once!"

The words cut Sena deep realizing Digby's mother did not approve of her courtship with Digby.

Sena thinks, *"Digby is a saloon owner? And his mother frowns up actresses?"* Her eyes fill with light stinging liquid as Mrs. Randaldt is her gossiping about her. She hides behind a display as they exit the mercantile.

As she approaches the counter, the clerk wraps her items in yesterday's newspaper. Sena notices an advertisement: Randaldt & Moss Saloon. D. Randaldt and P. Moss.

Digby's had never been mentioned his profession in their strolls or dinners. She decides departing Deadwood is a must. Mrs. Randaldt seems intent on squashing their blooming relationship. As she leaves the Franklin Hotel, she hands the hotel clerk a farewell letter addressed to Digby.

## Wine Room Law

The Wine Room Law in Montana, particularly through Sections 530, 534, and 537 of the state's penal code, dramatically reshaped the theater and entertainment industry in the early 1900s. The law prohibited theaters, playhouses, and variety halls from operating on Sundays and barred them from selling or furnishing liquor during performances. More significantly, it forbade the employment of women in these establishments if alcohol was involved—whether as musicians, waitresses, or performers. These restrictions directly impacted venues such as The Gem, The Topic, and The Globe, which thrived on a mix of theatrical entertainment and alcohol sales. Proprietors found themselves at odds with the law, as the financial viability of their establishments depended on both ticket sales and the lucrative business of liquor service. Actors and actresses, especially female performers, faced dwindling employment opportunities, forcing many to seek work outside Montana or within underground entertainment circles.

For actresses and proprietors alike, the law reinforced the broader societal movement to regulate morality in public entertainment spaces. Women, in particular, bore the brunt of these restrictions, as their mere presence in drinking establishments was increasingly associated with immorality. Authorities, emboldened by national temperance movements, cracked down on theaters and saloons suspected of violating the law, often equating female performers with "lewd women" if they were found near drinking patrons. This legislative push mirrored efforts in other Western states, such as Texas, where wine rooms became targets of police raids. However, in Montana, the outright prohibition of female employment in any liquor-connected venue marked an even stricter attempt to control the social order. The law signaled a broader cultural shift, where vice was defined not just by alcohol consumption but by the presence of women in spaces where men gathered to drink. This crackdown on wine rooms and entertainment halls foreshadowed the coming wave of Prohibition, setting a precedent for moral policing that would continue to shape public life in the American West.

## December 1905, Seattle, Washington: Meets Noel Adair

Christmas 1905 ~ Seattle

A Christmas unlike any I've ever known. No snow, no biting cold that burns the nose — just a damp sort of chill that settles into your bones. But the company makes up for the lack of winter's proper touch. Actors and actresses gathered in grand spirits, dressed in their finest, laughing, telling stories, reciting lines as if the entire night were a grand stage performance. I had forgotten how much I missed that world, the energy of it all, the way words seem to hold more magic when spoken by those who live to enchant.

And then, Noel.

Thought his name was fitting around the Christmas season. I thought he was joking when he introduced himself as Noel.

His name really is Noel Adair.

A projectionist, Noel refers to himself, a man whose hands coax moving pictures onto the screen. I had never thought much about the fellows behind the curtain, the ones who made the magic work. But there he was, easy on the eyes, quick with a smile, and entirely too sweet for his own good. Or for mine.

We fell into conversation, his voice steady, sure, speaking of things that seemed outlandish. "One day," he says, eyes glinting with certainty, "you'll sit in your own parlor and watch moving pictures. No need for the theater."

I laugh at the very idea. "That would take all the fun out of it," I tell him. "The grand halls, the laughter, the hush just before the reel begins."

But he only smiled. "It'll happen. Come see me when we're old—you'll owe me a dollar."

A bet I gladly take, for what are the odds of such a thing? Then again, the world is changing faster than I can keep track. Perhaps I should start tucking away my coins just in case.

For now, though, I'll settle for the magic of tonight. The laughter, the warmth, the glow of lights flickering against polished glass. A Christmas spent in a place I never expected to be, with people I never expected to meet. Life is full of surprises, and I find I don't mind them so much.

## April 1906, Coeur d'Alene, Idaho

April 1906 – Coeur d'Alene, Idaho

The news of the San Francisco earthquake and fire arrived today, and my heart aches for the countless lives lost. The devastation is unimaginable, and I cannot help but wonder how many souls have been swallowed by the chaos, their names never to be known again.

And now, I fear my mother is among them — not in life, but in the erasure of her last resting place. Detective Motts had written that he was close to solving the mystery of her death.

I had dared to hope for answers, for closure, but now, with the city in ruins, will the city's destruction forever hide the truth? The city's destruction likely reduced her grave to ash. Perhaps I will never know what truly happened to her.

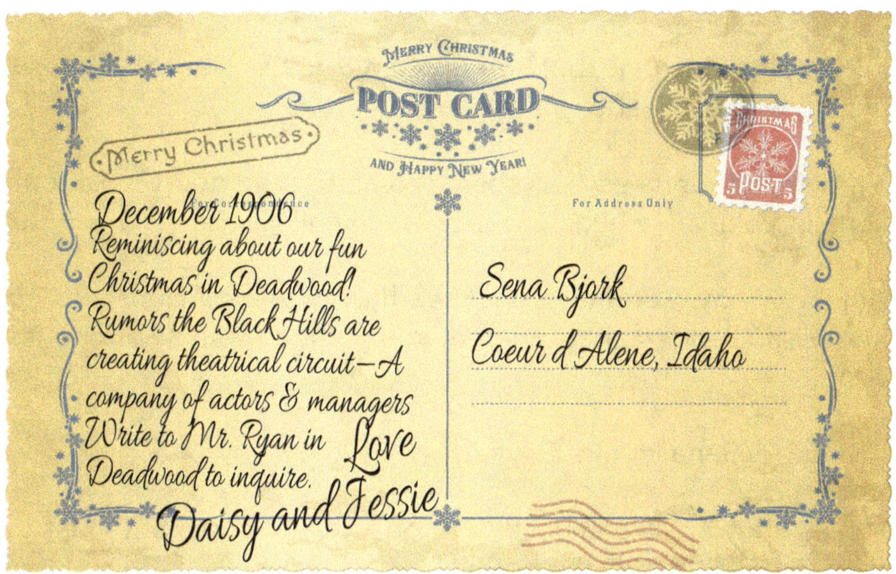

*Deadwood Theatre Co.*

## December 1906, Coeur d'Alene, Idaho

After Daisy and Jessie Kennison inform Sena of the newly forming Black Hills Vaudeville Circuit, Sena writes to Mr. Ryan at the Deadwood Theatre Company, Deadwood, South Dakota. While this Circuit seems appealing, she wrestles with the idea of being near Digby Randaldt again. She receives a better offer on a another vaudeville circuit with more travel opportunity which excites Sena! She continues as an actress traveling other vaudeville circuits.

## July 3, 1907, Missoula, Montana

The train ride was long, but Sena's heart is full as she anticipates reuniting with old friends in Missoula.

"OH, Hi Mary!" Sena says as she steps across the depot's platform embracing Mary in a hug. "Where are the children?"

"With the nanny. Goodness, it is dreadful hot this summer. Let's go to the Missoula Mercantile and get you outfitted with a Kimono for the 4th."

"A kimono?" Sena laughs playfully.

"Oh, yes, they are breathable! Comfortable and cool!" Says Mary. "The cooler the shade, the better!"

"How intriguing!" Sena brushes the sweat off her forehead and looking up, "the clouds appear glum today. Perhaps it will rain."

"Oh, heavens pour down on me!" Mary says theatrically, holding her hands out. "We also need to purchase bunting and decorations for our 4th of July celebration."

Sena affirms, "Oh, yes!" Climbing into the carriage with Mary. "How are the renovations coming along for the The Gem?"

"Dandy!" Mary smiles. "We are now equipped as a hotel, café and grill!" Looking down at her skirt, Mary pats it, her excitement waning. "The theater atmosphere isn't what it used to be." Now we are more socially moral. We have a new sign. Lifting her hand to spell out the words, "complete with a ladies' entrance!" she says snarkily.

Sena jokes, "Oh my, we would not want a lady to enter a restaurant unaccompanied through the front entrance!"

Mary laughs, "Law abiding is for the best for us all. The Tivoli Theatre is struggling, rumors of mischief and mayhem. Depending on where you are— you need to be careful traveling the circuit." Mary locks eyes staring into Sena's intensely.

An uncomfortable silence lasted a few minutes. Mary changes the subject, "Let's go in and get some supplies, shall we?"

Following their shopping trip, the carriage takes them from the mercantile, stopping at The Gem's hotel. Sena begins climbing out of the carriage. "You and Mr. Pierce should really look into one of those motor carriages—what is it called? Automobile."

Mary agrees and smiles, "Yes, we should, indeed. I will see you in the morning for the parade festivities."

A heavy downpour starts! Melodious laughter filled the air from both Mary and Sena. "Let the rain wash over me!" Sena cries, arms open wide.

**July 4, 1907, Missoula, Montana**

Sena looks at the clock in The Gem Café, 8:45 am. She takes the last bite of her triangular toast with butter and heads outside The Gem Hotel. Rain showers from the evening before cooled the atmosphere kept the dust minimal. The sky was brightly lit and the sunshine's glow made the city look magical to Sena.
The streets were alive with the energy of people and floats assembling for the parade. While she passed by, the Eagles were putting together their parade float. The sight of the Eagles gathering reminding her of Owen, Spider, and Digby. All of them fellow Eagle members. Her former male companions. They are all so different, yet had this in commonality. Complex emotions stir inside her, making her stomach a bit queasy.

Sena watches as people scurry to and fro their floats, placing the finishing touches before the festivities begin at 10 am. She sees the Pierces a short distance ahead. Sporting his derby, Mr. Pierce and the elegant Mary, with their children, were a sight to behold. Stateliness and propriety were evident in the new nanny, whom Mary had spoken so well of. Sena energetically waves to get their attention.

As they watch the parade, Mary mentions to Sena that Mrs. S. Fay has opened a new beauty parlor at the Hotel Rankin.

Sena asks, "Does she offer new types of beauty services?"

Mary readjusting Fern's bow, "Yes. For white flakes on the scalp—what is it called?"

"For Dandruff?" Sena inquires.

Mary smiles as she waves to someone on a float. "Yes, dandruff and thinning hair. Some won't go to her beauty parlor, but I tell them Mrs. Fay is superb!"

The Pierce children's eyes were wide with wonder as colorful floats passed by, music filling the air with infectious energy. Little hands eagerly waved at performers, and giggles escaped as clowns made funny faces. The joy radiating from the Pierce children was a sight to behold, a pure and unfiltered display of youthful exuberance that spread smiles to all those around them. Their enthusiasm during the parade was a reminder of the simple pleasures that bring light to even the dullest of days.

Veterans of the local Typographical Union walk with canes in their hands. They wore long linen dusters and white hats as a uniform; perfect light clothing for a hot summer day. The firecracker on the float was enormous. Some of their printers were also dressed in red, representing devils.

The final 25 vehicles of the parade were automobiles. Sena ponders about how all those motors work. What a delight! A roar, a whiz, a flash, engines.

Frank Pierce adds, chuckling, "Tonight, there will be double the amount of vehicles zooming around Missoula. The speed ordinance will be temporarily suspended so they can whiz around! I can't wait to see it!"

*"I have had more fun than going to the circus. Watching the youngsters operate the machine. And I guess they have had more fun than I have."*

-Franklin J. Pierce
*The Missoulian,* May 3, 1907

Mary adds, "The Missoula Eagles Band will play the Court House Square this evening, too. Sure to be a treat. Let's go back to the house. Sena, you are in for a fun surprise!"
Sena smiles.

Missoula looks up at Sena bouncing up and down as she walks, "A merry-go-round! PaPa installed it in our yard!"

Mary smiles. "Frank had it installed in May."

The Pierce children on the merry-go-round, Missoula, Montana.

Frank adds, "I have had more fun than going to the circus. Watching the youngsters operate the machine. And I guess they have had more fun than I have."

Mary adds, "Yes, and it's enjoyable for the entire neighborhood." At the Pierce home, Sena watches the children whirl around on the merry-go-round, their laughter rising above the steady hum of music from the music-box machine. Joy radiates from them, unrestrained and infectious. In the distance, the river glimmers, adding to the idyllic scene—one she commits to memory.

And it is Frank Pierce who made it happen—not just for his own children, but for the entire neighborhood. He was right. Watching these young ones be so carefree is every bit as delightful as attending a circus. As the sun dipped below the horizon, Sena leisurely walks back to the hotel, mesmerized by the dazzling fireworks lighting up the sky. The colorful rockets soar high above Water-Works Hill to the north, painting the darkness with brilliant balls of light and scattering sparks. With booming cannons and playful crackers, the air echoed. A hint of gunpowder hung in the air, heightening the moment's thrill.

Sena hums and mumbles under her breath, "Cannons boom and crackers pop!"

**Sena thinks, "This is what pure joy looks like."**

September 1907, Billings, Montana

The last year or so has been another whirlwind traveling the circuit. I've occasionally popped back over to Missoula to sing at The Gem when Mr. Pierce needs a fresh act or has an open slot. It's comforting to know I still have a place there, though I wonder how much longer I will keep up this pace.

Mr. Pierce is making a lot of changes. He has bought a café in Missoula and is combining it with the theater to make a hotel, café, and theater. He's always building on and changing things up.

Frank Gates — dear, ridiculous Frank — has landed himself a manager's post at the Topic Theatre here in Billings. He wrote, urging me to visit, promising a lively town and a good stage. Curiosity got the better of me, and so here I am. I haven't seen Frank in a long time now he's gone and gotten himself married. I am anxious to meet his new wife, though I can't quite picture him as a settled man.

He tells me he's trying to implement many of the entertainment business principles that Mr. Pierce and Davenport put into practice at The Gem — strong variety, reliable acts, and making sure the audience gets their money's worth. I hope for his sake that Billings embraces it. A town's taste for entertainment can be fickle.
Tomorrow, I'll see the Topic Theatre for myself.

Mid-performance at the Topic Theatre, a commotion erupts near the entrance. The doors burst open as a flood of actors and actresses from the Globe Theatre rush inside, their faces pale with urgency.

"Get out! All of you!" A woman gasps, breathless. "Sheriff's on his way! Any woman caught in here will be arrested!"

Confusion ripples through the crowd. Sena freezes, her heart hammering in her chest.

Mrs. Gates' (Frank's wife) eyes widen in terror. "We better run before the sheriff gets here!" She whispers fiercely. Sena lifts the sides of her skirt to run. She flees out the side door, feet pounding against the dirt alley.

"Stop right there!" A sheriff's deputy shouts at her and others.

She pushes harder, breath ragged, weaving through Billings' darkened streets. She is not familiar with the city's layout. The pounding of boots behind her spur her onward. Ahead, the flickering glow of lanterns make the streets seem endless. Desperation claws at her chest.

A horse trough looms ahead. Without thinking, she ducks underneath it, pressing herself into the damp ground. The reek of wet wood fills her nose. She clenches her fists, willing herself to be still.

A tickling sensation crept up her arm. A spider. She bites her lip, swallowing a whimper.

Boots stomp past the gravel grinding. "Did she go this way?" one voice shouts.

"Damn if I know. Just another actress, anyway. There's more to find." Says the officer.

Time elapses before she dares move. When she feels certain the coast was clear, she creeps out, dusts herself off, and sprints toward her boarding house. Miss Malla Goad meets her at the door, eyes sharp with concern.

The next morning, Miss Goad says, "Have you seen the newspaper?" She whispers, pulling Sena inside. "This Wine Room Law is getting serious. I'll do my best to hide you. Maybe the sheriff won't know you since you're new in Billings."

Sena sinks into a chair, breath still coming fast, "Wine Room Law?" she gasps.

Miss Goad sighs, setting a newspaper in front of her. "Read it yourself. Women are being fined a hundred dollars, sometimes jailed for a month. Just for being inside a theater where liquor's sold. Mrs. Gates was arraigned. She had some choice words for the lawmen, from what I hear."

Sena ran a shaky hand through her hair. She thinks, "*Why have I been so foolish? Frank Gates must have known how dangerous it is here for women to be actresses.*"

Her mind reels back to Mr. Pierce. The café. The hotel rooms. The removal of the bar. He probably knew the dangers long ago before the rest of us did. Knowing Pierce, he struggled with the changes, yet his business aspirations led him to have the best reputable business. This also, why they insisted I travel on the Texas circuit a few years prior. It clicks in her mind, Frank and Mary were aiming to protect her.

She swallows hard. Maybe it was time to leave the stage. This business—this life—was becoming too chaotic and too dangerous. That night, by lantern light, she pens a letter to her old roommate, Greta, still in Butte.

With trembling hands, she sealed the envelope, wondering if this was truly the end of her life on the stage.

## October 1907, Butte, Montana

Sena adjusts the lace cuff of her sleeve as she steps onto the trolley, Greta settling in beside her. The ride home from the dog show was filled with cheerful conversation—Greta still gushing about the Boston terrier she had nearly smuggled home in her coat, while Sena was slightly crestfallen that Mrs. Stevenson's Dalmatian had not taken the top prize. The trolley's familiar jostling was almost soothing, the hum of the city surrounding them.

And then she sees him. Digby. He is seated near the middle of the trolley, one arm draped casually over the back of the seat, but when his eyes meet hers, his posture straightens, his expression shifting from surprise to something softer. Something unreadable.

Greta looks between them, her lips twitching in amusement. "Well, well," she murmurs under her breath before settling back into her seat, leaving Sena no choice but to approach him.

"Digby," she says, clasping her hands in front of her. "What brings you to Butte?"

His blue eyes search hers, as if gauging whether her question was one of mere politeness or genuine interest. "Business," he says. "I'm looking into a new show horse."

Sena smiles, unsure what else to say. Their past is still an open wound, but there he was, as if the years between them had never passed by.

"I'd like to catch up," he continues. "Would you join me for dinner?"

She hesitates. Every rational thought tells her to refuse the invitation. Their relationship had ended abruptly. A small part of her still wonders what could have been. She exhales, "Alright. Dinner."

Napton Café was the picture of elegance. A Flemish scroll oak pattern framed the walls, their buff and brown tones illuminated by soft electric lights. Sena smoothed her skirts as she took in the fine linens and polished silverware. She hadn't expected Digby to take her somewhere so grand.

"Where are you staying in Butte?" She asks patting her lips with the cloth napkin.

"The Finlen," he awkwardly fidgeted with his napkin. And then he blurts "I want you to marry me."

Sena freezes, her fork poised midair. Half choking on her food and sitting her fork down, she drops her cloth napkin on her lap. Picking up the napkin, she meet his gaze, steady and certain. "Digby… what are you saying?"

"I was a fool." He reached for her hand, his voice thick with conviction. "I know *why* you left."

She swallows forming a lump in her throat. "This is sudden."

Digby continues, "When you left, rumors circulated about you leaving hastily. It must be because I own a saloon."

"Digs, you were not honest with me. Why did you keep this from me?" Sena asks.

"I was afraid you would think of me as a bad man, a deficit in moral living." Digby adds.

Her heart and head battle, ready for war. She thinks, "*Can I trust him? Can I trust myself? He knows nothing about my divorce to Owen. I should tell him. No, I am a fair maiden. This is a new start. Saloons are all over the west, it's not that bad. Anna DeKoven married a saloon owner. Wait, that ended badly. Frank Pierce served alcohol, and he is not a bad man, right?*

But in that moment, she sees the sincerity in his eyes, the way his large fingers tighten slightly over her dainty hands, as if afraid she would slip away again.

And she hears herself say it. "Yes."

Sena nearly ran home, the excitement bubbling in her chest as she burst through the door.

"Greta! Greta, you won't believe—"Sena exclaims.

Greta looks up from her knitting, one brow arched. "What's got you in such a state?"

Sena catches her breath. She beams. "Digby asked me to marry him."

Greta's needles still. "And?"

"I says yes!" Sena laughs, hugging herself. "Betrothed, Me! Oh, Greta, I think—I think this is right."

But before Greta could respond, frantic knocking at the door interrupts the moment.

A young man, barely more than a boy, stands breathless on the stoop. "Miss Bjork?"

"Yes?" Her stomach twists.

"Miss Digby Randaldt. He—he's been in an accident. A carriage collision. He's been taken to the St. James Hospital."

The room spun.

## St. James Hospital, Butte, Montana

The hospital smells of antiseptic and something far worse—desperation. Sena sits uneasy in the hallway, her hands clench in her lap, barely noticing when a man approaches

"Sena."

She looks up. It's Digby's brother, Dexter she wonders. "Dexter...?" she had never met him, yet he resembles Digby.

"I came from the hotel as soon as I heard," he says, his tone clipped but not unkind.

A silence stretches between them. Trying to make small talk, she asks, "How is your mother?"

His hesitation was answer enough. "She's gone."

Sena feels the blood drain from her face. "Gone?"

"Passed away last winter." Dexter's voice was neutral.

Her pulse pounds in her ears. She blurts, "Did Digby only propose because she's gone?" and then covered her mouth not meaning to utter those words aloud.

Dexter met her gaze evenly, scoffing and grinning. "Only Digs can answer that. Our mother was a force to be reckoned with. When I married Neva, we eloped. Mother was furious." His eyes widen like Digby.

She feels as if the floor has dropped from beneath her. She is convinced Digby only asked her because his mother had passed away.

And then the doctor steps into the hall, his face grim.

"Are you with Mr. Randaldt?" He asks gently.

Sena and Dexter both stand nodding.

The doctor firmly says, "You should prepare yourself. He might not make it through the surgery."

The world blurred. She presses a hand to her mouth.

She had just says yes to his proposal—and now, she might lose him forever.

**Back to January 1948, California**

The sun hangs low over the city, smearing gold and crimson across the sky, its last rays flickering through the windows of Sena's Spanish-style bungalow. The white stucco walls and red-tiled roof stood out against the deepening dusk, while wrought iron details cast long, artistic shadows. Inside, the scent of roasted lamb and fresh-baked bread mingled with the tang of citrus from the kitchen. Sena fusses with the china, adjusting a fork a hair's breadth, her nerves a tightly wound spool. Everything had to be just so.
She paces across the terracotta tiles, her heels clicking in a sharp rhythm. Every detail had been seen to—the menu, the seating, even a little script of polished lines tucked away in her mind. Hollywood has trained her well. If she could handle directors barking orders and a hot set with a dozen takes, she can handle a Swedish Count and Countess at her dinner table. At least, that's what she tells herself.

Her dress—a knockout crimson number—hugs her in all the right places. It is classy, sure, but with just enough zip to make a statement. After all, this isn't some dull country club affair. This is her home, her life, and tonight, she isn't about to let jitters get the best of her.

The doorbell chimes, slicing through the hush. Show time.

She inhales deeply, smoothing a palm over her skirt before she answers the door. The Count and Countess stand there like they'd stepped out of a glossy magazine—poised, polished, and every bit as regal as their titles suggest. Sena flashes her best smile, one part warmth, two parts confidence.

"Count, Countess, welcome! It's a real treat to have you here." The Count returns her smile, his refined features softening with genuine charm. "Thank you, Sena. Your invitation is most appreciated."

The Countess nods, taking in the home with a keen eye. "Such a lovely space—there's a warmth to it. It speaks of good taste." Sena's stomach untangles just a little. Maybe tonight would go off without a hitch after all.

As the evening unfolds, the dining room buzzes with easy conversation. The wine flows, the courses arrived like clockwork, and laughter punctuate the air. Among the guests sat a well-known painter, Dorothy Visu Andersen, a few high-society types, and a diplomat who knows how to work a room. But it was the Count and Countess who held Sena's attention.

Between bites of braised beef and sips of a smooth Bordeaux, she finds herself watching, measuring their reactions. She ponders, *"Had they enjoyed the meal? Did they find the company engaging?"* She needn't have worried. The Count seemed right at home, and the Countess—graceful and self-assured—leaned in with interest whenever Sena spoke.

And then, just like that, the night took a turn she hadn't seen coming.

After the last course, the Count sits down his glass, his gazes steady. "Sena, your hospitality is unmatched. We would love for you and your husband to visit us in Sweden. It would be an honor."

Sena's breath hitches. Sweden. An invitation. A real one.
Sena's voice is shaky in surprise. "Sweden? You would have us?"

The Countess meets her gaze, her expression sincere. "You have a spirit, a warmth, that is rare. We look forward to welcoming you into our home."

She darts a glance at her husband. He, ever steady, smiled as if it were the most natural thing in the world. "We'd be honored, Count."

Sena barely hears the rest of the conversation. It all blurs into a happy haze—the clinking of glasses, the low hum of jazz from the record player, the easy flow of chatter.

She had come from nothing. Scraping by, counting pennies, chasing dreams that sometimes seemed out of reach. And now, Swedish royalty want her at their table.

She takes it all in—the glittering candlelight, the refined laughter, the way the evening had unfolded like something out of a picture show. If someone had told her years ago that she'd be here, in this moment, she would've called them screwy.

But here she was.

What a reverie.

## Preview of Book 3: *Sable & Gold*

As one chapter closes, another glimmers on the horizon...

The year is 1907, and Sena finds herself once again at a crossroads. Digby's fate hangs in the balance—will he survive the surgery? And if he does, will their love be enough to carry them into a shared future?

Set against the windswept grit and grandeur of the Black Hills of South Dakota, *Sable & Gold* explores the tension between yearning and destiny, fortune and fidelity. As the new century unfolds and the 1910s reshape the American West, Sena is drawn into fresh circles and unforeseen choices. Is she finally settling into the woman she was meant to be—or still reaching?

As the Great War casts its long shadow, Sena's path turns outward. Embracing a spirit of civic duty, she throws herself into service with the American Red Cross, finding purpose amid uncertainty. Through bandages, letters, and quiet leadership, she joins a generation of women reshaping their world—one selfless act at a time.

Spanning from 1907 to 1918, with reflections from 1930, this third installment in the Sagacity Stories Series delves deeper into the heart of a woman shaped by loss, resilience, and the gleam of something more. Will love strike gold—or will it vanish like a shadow at dusk?

# Appendix

# CHARACTER GLOSSARY

## Fictional Characters

Characters invented to create historic fiction novel series. They are based upon inspiration from historic research.

**Noel Adair,** projectionist of moving pictures, Seattle, Washington.

**Alvina Synnova "Sena" Bjork**, main character.

**Owen Bockley**, comedic vaudeville actor, Sena's husband in Book 1, *Zoetic Solace*. Disappears after 11 days of marriage.

**Greta Clark**, Sena's friend and roommate in Butte.

**Esmie Fenwick,** co-worker of Sena and Greta's at Paumie's Dye House.

**Malla Goad,** Landlady in Billings.

**Annalie Leutner,** Sena's mother, resided San Francisco, California.

**Henry Leutner,** Sena's stepfather, resided Helena.

**Emma Leutner,** Sena's half sister. St. Vincent's Academy, Helena.

**Carah Leutner,** Sena's half-sister. Vincent's Academy, Helena.

**Christian "Christie" Leutner,** brother to Henry Leutner, proprietor of a saloon in Butte. Former love interest of Annalie Leutner in Book 1.

**Edith "Edie" Leutner,** Sena's half-sister. Vincent's Academy, Helena.

**Cecilia "Cici" Maley,** bookbinder, Helena. Former head domestic servant at Martin M. Holter home.

**Detective Motts,** detective from the San Francisco Police Department.

**Dexter Randaldt,** Brother of Digby Randaldt.

**Digby Randaldt,** Sena's love interest in Deadwood, South Dakota.

**Safronna Randaldt,** widow of Amos Randaldt. Mother to Digby and Dexter. Lives in Deadwood, South Dakota.

**Marie Sanderlin,** friend and schoolmate of Sena's from Helena.

**Tipple Stett,** (dog) John "Spider" Stett's dog.

**Yara** (cat), Sena's cat in 1948.

# True, Unchanged Names - Characters

The names below, as recorded historically, are preserved in their original forms. Fictional dialogue has been included by the author to shape the narrative of this historical novel. The author's dialogue combines factual interpretation with creative invention to connect the story's gaps.

**Ashley Basco,** a well-known theater director and stage manager. Replaces William Davenport at The Gem in Missoula.

**Dr. John T. Brown,** Physician and Surgeon, Rogers Block, Missoula.

**Frank B. Carroll,** vaudeville actor. Married to actress, Gloie Eller.

**William E. Carroll,** Attorney, 527 Hennessy Bldg, Butte.

**William "Davy" Davenport,** actor and stage manager at The Gem Theatre. Civil War Veteran. Originally from Boston, Massachusetts.

**Anna DeKoven,** Vaudeville performer. Anna DeKoven is her stage name. Her real name is Anna Hoefer. Marries George Nink, Missoula..

**Gloie Eller,** Vaudeville actress and singer. Pronounced Glow-EEY. Married to comedian and actor, Frank B. Carroll. Originally from Zanesville, Ohio.

**Mrs. S. Fay,** beauty shop, Missoula.

**Frank S. Gates,** an Irish comedian on the Vaudeville circuit. Pictured on page 18.

**Albert J. Gibson,** architect, 2nd Floor of the Gibson Block, Missoula.

**Dr. Russel Gwinn,** Oculist (ophthalmologist) and Aurist (ear nose and throat doctor), Missoula.

**Albert "Red" Hall,** bartender Central Saloon, Missoula.

**Charles H. Hall,** Missoula County Attorney.

**Ella Knowles Haskell,** divorce attorney for Sena's mother. Friend of Sena's high school teacher Sarepta Sanders. Haskell was the first female lawyer in the state of Montana.

**William Hayes,** Missoula District Court Judge.

**Emily Holter,** wife of Martin. Former caretaker of Sena. Resident of Berkeley, California and Helena, Montana.

**Martin Holter,** husband of Emily. Resident of Berkeley, California and Helena, Montana.

**Milton Holter,** son of Martin and Emily Holter. Student at University of California, Berkeley.

**Charles E. Hollingsworth,** Chief of Police, Missoula.

**Dave Kelsey,** The Gem electrician, who runs the lighting and special effects for the theater.

**Daisy & Jessie Kennison,** fraternal twin sisters, Vaudeville performers.

**Frank Lichti,** cigar maker, Missoula.

**Emma Lichti,** wife of Frank Lichti.

**Zeta Lovell,** vaudeville singer.

**John MacGuire,** stage manager, Butte.

**Thomas C. Marshall,** attorney at law, partner at Marshall & Stiff, National Bank Building, 2nd Floor, Missoula.

**Ed Martin,** Undersheriff, Missoula County.

**Dr. William P. Mills,** general physician, First National Bank Building, 3rd Floor. Lived at Hotel Florence, Missoula.

**George Nink,** Louvre, saloon owner, Missoula. Marries Anna Hoefer, stage name: Anna DeKoven.

**Julia O'Neil,** actress, Frank Pierce's ex-wife, mother to Hartwell Pierce. Lived in Butte and Missoula, Montana when married to Frank. Returned to the United States living in Hamilton, Montana.

**Hartwell Pierce,** son of Franklin J. Pierce and Julia O'Neil. Born in Montana. After his parents divorce, his mother takes him to her native country of Ireland. Hartwell returns circa 1900 to Montana to live with his father and step-mother. Pictured on page 124.

**Francis "Frank" Edwin Pierce,** son of Percy Prescott Pierce. Similar in age to Hartwell Pierce. *Note: Not related to Franklin J. Pierce family.* Lives in Missoula.

**Franklin J. Pierce,** Proprietor of The Gem Theatre, Missoula. See extended biography in the appendix. Pictured on pages 141, 228, 237, 238 and 239.

**Franklin J. Pierce, Jr.,** son of Franklin J. and Mary Pierce. Born July 1903 in Missoula. Pictured on page 141, 237 and 239.

**Mary Helena Murphy Pierce,** Stage name: Mae Helena Brandon. Wife of Frank Pierce. Together they have Missoula, Fern and Frank, Jr. See extended biography in the appendix for more information. Pictured on pages 141, 233, 234, 237 and 239.

**Missoula "Pat" Pierce,** daughter of Franklin J. and Mary Pierce. Born 1901 in Missoula. Pictured on pages 203 and 237.

**Montana "Fern" Pierce,** daughter of Franklin J. and Mary Pierce. Born 1902 in Missoula. Pictured on pages 203 and 237.

**Percy Prescott Pierce,** owner of Hotel Missoula which is at the corner of Stevens and Main. His wife is also named Mary. *Note: Not related to Franklin J. Pierce family.*

**Sheriff Clarence R. Prescott,** Missoula.

**John Quong,** Chinese merchant, Missoula.

**Michael "Mike" Reinig,** friend of Martin Holter. Employer of Henry Leutner. A mercantile/grocer, 101 E. State, Helena 1895.

**Madame Marie Paumie Rimboud,** (1857-1942)—owner of Paumie's Parisian Dye House, Butte Montana. Marie, originally from Paris, France first immigrated to New York. Then establishing a Parisian dye house and dry cleaners in Butte, Montana. One of a kind!

**Rev. Frederick J. Salsman,** reverend at the Emmanuel Baptist Church, Missoula.

**Manuel Samayoa,** acrobatic aerialist from Spain. Married to Cleo Samayoa.

**Cleo Samayoa,** vaudeville dancer.

**Sarepta M. Sanders,** Sena's high school teacher in Helena.

**John R. "Spider" Stett,** retired puglist/boxer and bartender at The Gem Theatre, Missoula. Also works for William Yerrick, Garden City Brewery Company and Bottling Works. Originally from Ireland.

**Henry C. Stiff,** attorney at law, partner at Marshall & Stiff, National Bank Building, 2nd Floor, Missoula.

**Blanche "Lulu" Sutton,** actress. Daughter of Richard "Dick" Perry Sutton, Sutton's Theatre, Butte.

**Maud Templeton,** Vaudeville actress.

**Thomas Thibedeau,** owner, Central Saloon, Democratic City Delegate, Missoula.

**Harry W. Thompson,** Missoula County Sheriff.

**Galen "Curly" Williamson alias, Curly Williams,** bartender, multiple cities in Montana.

**William Yerrick,** proprietor of the Garden City Bottling Company, Missoula.

**Zetta Yerrick,** William Yerrick's daughter.

# Franklin J. Pierce
# Entrepreneur, showman and risk-taker

Of the four real-life individuals named Frank—woven into this work of historical fiction, Franklin J. Pierce holds one of the most prominent roles. As the owner of The Gem, he becomes a cornerstone in Sena's journey into Vaudeville, offering her both opportunity and direction. Alongside his wife Mary and their family, Franklin creates a refuge—a steady, welcoming haven amidst the turbulence of Sena's travels.

**Franklin J. Pierce**
**born James P. Harshaw**

You've already glimpsed Franklin's gift for lifting spirits, for turning ordinary evenings into moments of joy, but behind his charisma lies a past marked by hardship. Before The Gem, loss shadowed Franklin's life and repeated disappointment. The theater became his redemption—a stage not just for performers, but for healing. These were his glory years, where bringing smiles to others' faces offered him solace, perhaps even salvation.

What follows is my interpretation of the man behind the curtain— Franklin J. Pierce, as I imagine him, in all his light and sorrow. The first thing you need to know—he wasn't Franklin J. Pierce at all. His real name was James P. Harshaw.

Imagine an 1860s Texas sun hung low like a molten coin in the west, casting a bruised-orange sheen over the chaparral. Heat shimmered on the horizon, where mesquite trees stood gnarled and stubborn, clawing at a sky wide enough to swallow a man whole. Dust rose in lazy swirls from the trail, kicked up by hooves and boots, and settled on everything. The brims hats, rifle stocks, and the cracked lips of men who had learned not to speak unless they had something worth saying.

On the edge of a scorched prairie, a lone rider paused, silhouetted against the dying light. Captain Julius Harshaw, Wells Regiment Texas Calvary. His hat cast a shadow over sun-scoured cheeks, and a pistol hung heavy at his side. Behind him, the land stretched out like a worn prayer—hard, holy, and unforgiving. Ahead, a town waited. Not much more than a clutch of buildings huddled around a dry well and a sagging church bell, but it had a name and people, and that was enough to make it worth fighting for—or dying in. Whispers of war had become roars. Union or Confederacy—loyalty was no longer just a matter of opinion. It was a matter of survival. This was Texas in the sixties—caught between the past and the firestorm coming, proud and wounded, bold as a mustang and just as hard to break. December 1866, just before Christmas, he married Emeline Sewell they began their family in Fannin County, Texas. Life on their farm was rugged and strong. They had James, Rosa and John. Tragedy hit when Emeline died in 1870. James was a mere 5 years old when he lost his mother.

His father Julius remarried to a widow, Mary Serena Hughes Pierce, in March 1872. Mary's husband, a local physician, died as a result of a feud. A blended family was created by including her two sons, Hartwell and Willie Pierce. And soon a son together, Julius Harshaw, Jr.

Captain Harshaw's success on the land was hard won. With his steady hand, he amassed acres in both Fannin and Grayson Counties—land that, like the man himself, made no apologies. The earth was unforgiving, shaped by the weight of history. The wind carried the scent of creosote and blood—lingering echoes of old battles fought and forgotten. Tensions hung thick in the air, as persistent as the locusts that buzzed, clinging to the sparse, stubborn green that dared to grow. This was a land that demanded respect and offered little mercy in return.

In 1875, Texas was in the midst of a turbulent transformation. The fires of change burned hot as the Texas Constitutional Convention shaped a new political future. Railroads began to carve through the wilderness, pulling settlers, cattle, and promises of prosperity with them. The cattle drives exploded, pushing herds across vast stretches of land, but with the boom came the shadow of violence—Texas Rangers and local lawmen struggling to maintain order against the ever-growing threat of cattle rustlers. The air was thick with the clash of law and lawlessness.

It was on Sunday, October 24, 1875, when life would change forever for James. The sun was beginning to dip beneath the horizon as he sat down to supper with his family on their farm. The evening should have been like any other—quiet, warm, the comforting hum of a day's work drawing to a close. But the sharp rap of a knock on the door shattered the peace.

James, age 9, rose and walked toward the door. When he opened it, four men on horseback stood in the dimming light, their faces drawn and weary from travel. They claimed to be mere wanderers in need of rest for the night.

James ran back into the home to fetch his father. He reached for his father's hand, a sense of unease prickling at the back of his neck. Together, they made their way to the front porch, his father a few steps ahead, his worn boots creaking against the dry wooden floor.

Before James could fully understand what was happening, a gunshot split the air. The world around him seemed to slow, as his father, Julius Harshaw, crumpled before him. All of the men—now masks—one had fired the shot, then turned and fled into the night, leaving only the sound of hooves and the hot pulse of blood. Imagine the shock, the gut-wrenching terror, the unspeakable weight of watching your father fall, his life stolen in an instant. The men, it was later says, were cattle thieves—part of Jim Richards' notorious gang. James' father, Julius Harshaw had been set to testify against them in criminal court. His death was not a random act of violence—it was a silent execution, a brutal message sent that autumn evening.

James was only a boy—barely more than a child when his mother died. At the age of five, he had lost the woman who had given him life. Now, at age nine, he stood hand in hand with the one man who had raised him—only to lose him in a flash, his father's strong body crumpling before his eyes. His stepmother and a blended family of siblings remained, but James would forever carry the weight of that night, the sound of the shot ringing in his ears, the ghost of his father's presence haunting every step he took after.

Little is known about the remaining years of James' childhood, though whispers of hardship and rumors of abuse cloud the silence—nothing concrete, just shadows in the family's past. But the stories that have survived, passed down through the years, tell of family lore recounting how James and his brother, John, ran away to Fort Worth, Texas. There, they found themselves drawn into the chaotic world of a carnival and a gambling ring—fascinating yet dangerous, a place where the line between freedom and folly blurred.

John eventually returned to Texas, but James—always the restless one, always seeking the next horizon—set his sights on Montana, chasing the wild promise of adventure. It was there, among the rugged landscapes and untamed territories, that he reinvented himself. Gone was the boy who had lost everything. In his place stood Franklin James Pierce—or simply F.J. Pierce, the name that would follow him, the identity he would embrace as he stepped into a new life, far from the shadow of his past.

In 1890, James Harshaw, now known as Frank Pierce, found himself working as a waiter at Mellen's Restaurant in Helena, Montana. He also worked as a steward, the hospitality manager at the Cosmopolitan Hotel. He later worked for Emil & Joe's, a well-regarded restaurant where he gained his footing in the restaurant business.

In 1893, as autumn leaves began to fall, a shift in his life direction took place. Embracing the spirit of entrepreneurship, Frank entered a brief partnership with a French chef, Alex Bodini, and together they opened Maison Riche, a restaurant located inside the Windsor Hotel in Butte, at 19 E. Broadway.

The restaurant's menu reflected their ambition: from 6 am to 11 am patrons could enjoy ham, eggs, and potatoes for just 25 cents; a merchant's lunch was served from 11 am to 3 pm for 40 cents; and from 4 pm to 8 pm, guests could indulge in a French dinner. Also, they could order blue point oysters, fish, and fresh game. Yet, by November of the same year, their partnership dissolved, Ed Dillon bought out Alex Bodini's interest in the restaurant.

During Christmas 1893, a free Christmas dinner was provided by Pierce and Dillon to every messenger and paperboy in Butte, Montana. The newsboys reportedly showed great appreciation. Imagine the aroma of roasted turkey filled the room, enticing the hungry newsboys. It speaks to Pierce's spirit of giving and community gathering. Feeding these struggling boys warmed their hearts long after they'd eaten the pie, a simple act of kindness with lasting impact.

During this period, Frank became romantically involved with Julia O'Neil, an Irish actress who yearned to return to her homeland. Their relationship blossomed, and they welcomed a son, Hartwell. Soon after his birth, Frank and Julia married, marking a new chapter in his personal life.

By 1895, he was in Missoula running the Headquarters Saloon. There you could find entertainment while you dined. One fun tale is that for election day, November 1896, Pierce had arranged for special wires to come into the saloon so that results came directly to the patrons in real time. He was innovative in how to bring people together. Julia grew unhappy and took their son Hartwell to Ireland.

In 1897, Frank files for divorce from Julia and marries actress Lulu Inman. He opened The Gem as a saloon, originally. However,

MAE HELENA BRANDON

COMEDIENNE, VOCALIST, DANCER AND MALE IMPERSONATOR

WARDROBE FIRST CLASS
PHOTOS FOR LOBBY

PERMANENT ADDRESS
1302 MICHIGAN AVE CHICAGO

GENERAL BUSINESS

Work in

Acts,
Dramas,
Burlesque,
etc.

Character Work a Specialty

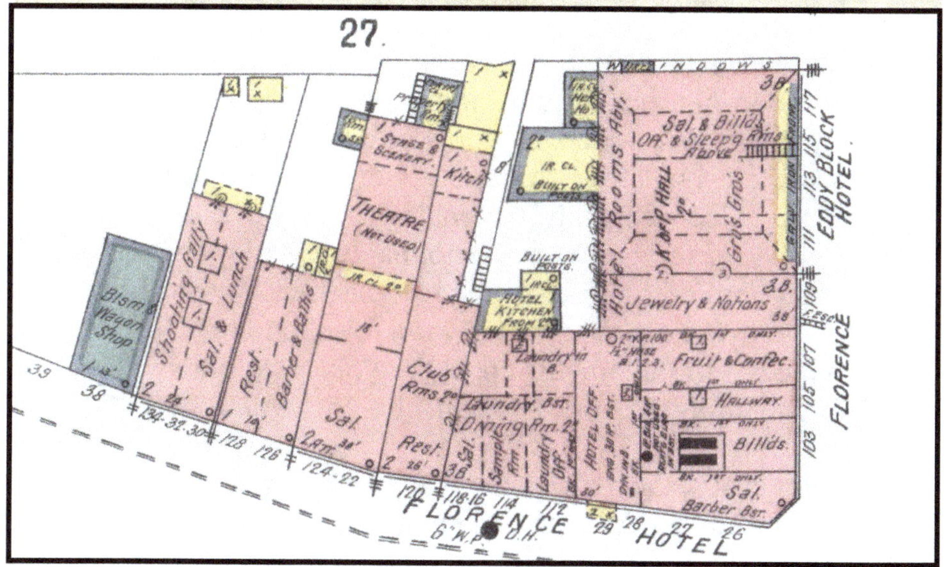


*West Front Street, Missoula, Montana, Sanborn Map, 1902. Library of Congress*

Entertainment was a part of the establishment. While The Gem starts small, it successfully grows into a great concert hall and theater. It did have its fair share of struggles with brushes with the law, gambling, etc.

Lulu continued on working vaudeville circuits. When Frank filed for divorce in 1900, she was working for the Rentz-Santly Burlesque & Novelty Co. That same year he met a true gem, his third and last wife, Mary Helena Murphy, who performed in his theater under the name Mae Helena Brandon.

**Mary Helena Murphy Pierce**

**Stage Name: Mae Helena Brandon**

Mary was an extraordinary performer! She began acting in the Texas vaudeville circuit around age eight, moving from New Orleans to San Antonio, Texas. Stage names included Little Belle Lyons and Mamie Goodrich. By adulthood he was a woman of remarkable versatility and boundless energy. She dazzled audiences as a comedienne, captivating them with her sharp wit, and her vocal performances were nothing short of mesmerizing. She graced both dramatic and comedic stages, showcasing her ability to move seamlessly between roles, and her dance performances—spanning multiple styles, including burlesque— captured the attention of every room she entered.

One of her unique talents was her skill in male impersonation, a craft she mastered with both charm and conviction. In the late 1890s, Chicago became her home base. After marrying Frank, her home became Missoula. A place where she could nurture her career while still raising a family. Hartwell, Frank's son from his marriage to Julia, returned from Ireland to the United States to live with his father and Mary. Hartwell created a close bond with his step-mother.

Despite her demanding schedule, Mary was deeply committed to family and theater alike. She was fortunate to have a nanny to assist her with the children and a housekeeper. She played a crucial role in scouting new acts and training the local stock players, ensuring that the theater maintained its high standards. While her professional life flourished, she never lost sight of her greatest joy—raising their 10 children, balancing the spotlight with the nurturing warmth of home. Around 1910, Mary's mother had come to live with them.

*Under the proprietorship of Frank J. Pierce, The Gem has become one of the cleanest, coziest, brightest theaters of its class in the West. The performances are refined and up-to-date, refreshing and devoid of all objectionable features and the most fastidious need not hesitate to pay it a visit.*

The Missoulian, September 7, 1902

As you've read in *Reaching for Reveries,* The Gem Theatre was more than just a place of entertainment—it was a vibrant hub of life, filled with laughter, music, and drinks. Performers from all corners of the country graced the stage in Missoula, and Frank and Mary

Pierce, along with their dedicated staff, worked tirelessly to elevate The Gem's reputation. They sought to combat the widespread view of vaudeville as crude or low-class, striving to present it as a refined, respectable form of entertainment that stood in stark contrast to the saloon girls and vice, often associated with the time.

The incident involving Gloie and Maud, who were falsely accused of stealing from a customer, actually took place and is rooted in real events, supported by court documents and eyewitness accounts. Their names were eventually cleared. Despite The Gem's occasional brushes with vice, Frank Pierce and William Davenport tirelessly worked to prove the two women's innocence, thus clearing their names and reputations. The commitment to integrity and fairness that Frank and his team displayed in this situation spoke to the values they upheld, even amidst the challenges of running a thriving entertainment establishment.

> *Owing to the great number of transient people expected in Missoula for the next few years, the proprietor of this house, Frank J. Pierce intends to immediately begin the remodeling of the same into a hotel for the entertainment of transient guests.*
>
> *The Missoulian, 1907*

However, the Montana Wine Room laws made it increasingly difficult to maintain business as usual. To comply with these new regulations, Frank had to adapt his operations. By 1907, he seized an opportunity to expand his influence, purchasing the Woodworth Café—formerly the Florence Hotel. His vision for the establishment was a complete transformation. Frank planned to convert it into a high-class hotel and dining venue, offering a refined space for both locals and travelers.

The new Gem Hotel, Café and Grill would feature dining rooms specifically for ladies, complete with private entrances and several intimate dining rooms on the second floor reserved for women and their escorts. This addition aimed to create a comfortable, respectable environment. The hotel renovations would also include an upgrade of the restaurant facilities and the installation of steam heating throughout the building. Frank's plans didn't stop there; he intended to continue offering musical performances and vaudeville entertainment, ensuring that guests of the hotel could enjoy high-quality shows each evening. He even had the legendary Al Jolson, one of the greatest vaudeville entertainers of his time, grace his stage!

By reimagining his business, Frank Pierce sought to redefine the intersection of

The Pierce Family with their nanny circa 1908. Left to right, Missoula; Mary posing with Virginia; The nanny holding Rose Catherine; Fern holding the hand of Franklin J. Pierce and Frank, Jr. The baby Rose Catherine Pierce died as an infant. She was born August 15, 1907 and died May 16, 1908 in Missoula.

entertainment and hospitality. He envisioned the hotel as a refined, family-friendly venue, shifting the focus away from alcohol to create a more upscale and inviting atmosphere. The extensive renovations, combined with the continuation of vaudeville performances, allowed him to challenge and reshape the boundaries of what was considered tasteful entertainment in the early 20th century.

On September 1, 1908 at 1 am, the curtain closed at The Gem for the last time. The employees presented Frank with a Howard watch to show the esteem they held in him.

The business eventually transformed into The Ye Olde Inn, a

new chapter that was tragically cut short by a devastating fire. When the flames subsided, Frank discovered that the insurance company refused to cover the losses, leaving him with little to rebuild. Following the insurance company's denial of the fire loss claim. Frank sat at the kitchen table in Missoula. A stack of money sat before Frank. Missoula exclaimed to her father, "That's a lot of money!"

Frank sadly responds, "This is the only money we have, Missoula." In search of a fresh start, Frank and Mary and their children relocated to Butte, Montana, where he took up bartending during the volatile days of Prohibition.

This line of work was fraught with danger, as the law cracked down on illegal alcohol sales. It's says that Frank may have resorted to paying bribes to local officials, looking the other way to keep his livelihood intact in a time when survival often meant navigating the shadows of the law. The risks he took during this period were as high as the stakes in his pursuit of a steady income—a testament to his resilience in the face of ever-changing and often unforgiving circumstances.

One could fill an entire book with stories from Frank's remarkable life. What follows is merely a glimpse into his world as a showman and risk-taker. Pierce was a visionary in the realm of vaudeville and entertainment—above all, he brought joy to the masses. In Missoula, that joy arrived in droves.

**Frank Pierce's Mustache Cup that he kept at the barber shop.**

Though he no longer appears at 11 am to stroll the streets for his daily shave—derby hat on his head, gold cane in hand, and a cigar typically pinched between his fingers—his presence still lingers. During his lifetime, he even kept a mustache cup at the barber shop, a small nod to his flair and fastidious nature. Frank Pierce left an indelible mark on the city.

Family photographs courtesy of Patricia McGrath Snipes, granddaughter of Frank and Mary Pierce.

# Author's Historical Notes and References

Several historic documents and archival material have been accessed over the last decade to culminate the research to write this historic fiction novel series. The bulk of the references are genealogical records. I would like to acknowledge the many librarians, archivists, curators, clerks at local government offices, who have assisted in my search for records regarding the characters included in this book. It is my sincere hope that this historical information provides the reader with not only context for the novel, yet also serves as a means for learning about the history of the setting. For local residents of the setting, may it be a celebration of their locale.

The careful blending of fact and fiction for the fictional narrative is complex. While every effort was made to verify factual information, the possibility of errors or omissions in the data cannot be ruled out. It is very much infused with a multitude of fiction.

The following sources including numerous newspaper articles too lengthy to list one by one were consulted during the inspiration and writing of this book:

City Directories 1900 to 1907
U.S. Federal Census, 1900, 1910, 1920, 1930, 1940, 1950
Primary Resource Documents and Records from across the United States and Sweden, such as but not limited to: Birth, Marriage, Church, Parrish, School, Cemetery, Death, Divorce, Land, Probate. For this book in particular, civil and criminal court cases were referenced.

- Newspapers.com
- Library of Congress
- Sanborn Maps, Library of Congress
- FamilySearch.org
- FindAGrave.com
- Montana State Historical Society Online Records
- Montana State Historic Preservation Office Records
- Swenson Swedish Immigration Research Center
- Swedish Parish Records

## About the Author

Jennifer Toelle, grew up in the Mid-Ohio Valley, and living her adult life in Central Kansas. She is a museum curator in a local history museum and owner of Janine Chellington Press. Jennifer has degrees in American Studies from Columbia College and in the Humanities from Tiffin University.

She resides there with her husband, children, and beloved cats. An avid traveler and genealogy enthusiast, Jennifer delights in exploring the world and uncovering its connections. She finds joy in connecting people, places, and things, often marveling at the intricate web of relationships that spans various domains. She loves etymology and discovering word origins. One of her true passions is designing publications.

She began her author journey by researching and writing *Kansas Wesleyan University's Pictorial History*, demonstrating her deep appreciation for the region's history and culture. Her love for storytelling and her academic background make her a captivating author and a valuable asset to her community.

Jennifer's other books include *Adopting the Forgotten: Women Edition. The Sagacity Stories (January 2025)*, Book 1: *Zoetic Solace (May 2025)* and Book 2: *Reaching for Reveries (May 2025)*.

# BOOK CLUB DISCUSSION QUESTIONS

## Vaudeville & Societal Norms

What was the ongoing stigma surrounding Vaudeville, especially in the Western states and towns?

Why do you think this form of entertainment was viewed with both fascination and disapproval?

How did class, gender, and regional identity shape public attitudes toward Vaudeville performers?

In what ways did Vaudeville serve as both an escape and a risk for those who pursued it?

## Women & Performance

What unique challenges did women face as actresses or performers during this period?

How did societal expectations shape or restrict their roles both on and off the stage?

How did Sena navigate these expectations in contrast to other female characters?

Actress Gloie Eller told Sena she was lucky to have Frank Pierce as a proprietor of The Gem. Explaining how many other concert hall owners only cared about the receipts and turning profits. If Sena did not have this support system, and was forced into prostitution, how would her life differed?

Do you feel that performance offered women empowerment—or a different kind of confinement?

## Laws & Social Implications

What were the social implications of Montana's Wine Room Law?

How did it affect women, especially those in vulnerable positions?

What does the law reveal about gender, morality, and control?

What role does the Women's Christian Temperance Union play in the characters lives?

Many concert hall and saloon owners like Frank Pierce struggled to maintain their livelihoods while the reform movement was gaining strength. Discuss him as a "criminal" and  a "hero" for fellow people in their profession.

## Grief & Personal Loss

Discuss Sena's grief throughout the novel. Which death do you think impacted her the most—and why?

How did she cope with her grief? Did you feel her way of handling loss was realistic or surprising?

In what ways did grief shape her decisions, relationships, or sense of self?

## Franklin J. Pierce – Legacy & Influence

After reading Franklin J. Pierce's biography in the appendix, why do you think he was so determined to bring joy through entertainment?

How do his life experiences inform his philosophy, and how did that influence others in the story?

**Characters & Their Paths**

Discuss Spider's relationship with the law. Was he a victim of circumstance, a product of the era, or something else entirely?

What complexities make him stand out as a character?

What do you think will happen to Digby? Did you pick up on any clues or foreshadowing in the book that suggest his fate?

Sena has not told Digby about her former marriage to Owen. Should she disclose her divorced status? Or keep it a secret?

Who was your favorite character and why? Was it someone expected—or did a lesser-known character resonate with you?

9 798990 604827